DEADLY
TREASURE HUNT

SOMMER SMITH

LOVE INSPIRED SUSPENSE
INSPIRATIONAL ROMANCE

LOVE INSPIRED® SUSPENSE
INSPIRATIONAL ROMANCE

Recycling programs
for this product may
not exist in your area.

ISBN-13: 978-1-335-59797-7

Deadly Treasure Hunt

Love Inspired
22 Adelaide St. West, 41st Floor
Toronto, Ontario M5H 4E3, Canada
www.LoveInspired.com

Printed in U.S.A.

But lay up for yourselves treasures in heaven,
where neither moth nor rust doth corrupt,
and where thieves do not break through nor steal.
—*Matthew* 6:20

To Aunt Doris and Uncle Pat because you have always supported me and lifted me up, both in my ambitions and in prayer. Thank you so much!

ONE

Jayde Cambrey arriving on Deadman's Cay Island was the last thing Caldwell Thorpe needed.

He had been working night and day to piece together the events leading up to his late wife, Natalie Farley's, death and prove it had been no accident. Her cousin's arrival was bound to complicate things. From what he had heard from the lawyers, she had already had plenty to say about his inheriting the island property, none of it positive. Add to that the fact that he and Jayde hadn't exactly gotten along the one time they had met and his stomach clenched with anxiety.

It wasn't just her presence causing his distress. Caldwell had felt as if a dark cloud had been hanging over him for the last several years, and he was more than ready to set his life to rights. A few years ago, his mother had reappeared in his life, setting him at odds with his brothers by his own refusal to forgive her for abandoning the family. He had left Wyoming in search of fulfillment in his law career and met Natalie at a summer gala in Nantucket while vacationing with a friend from law school. Natalie had been in Nantucket with a friend as well, though her family lived in Georgia. He had fallen for Natalie even before heading back to Key West, where he had set up temporary shop as an attorney. Learning he was living there, Natalie had persuaded him to meet her on Deadman's Cay later that summer at her family's vacation home, Rose Stone Cottage. It had cemented their relationship and they were soon engaged. They married six months later.

Remaining estranged from his family, Caldwell had moved to Rose Stone Cottage, where Natalie had always wanted to live year-round, and continued to practice law on Key West after they married. But soon she began to complain about his constant absence with cases. A friend mentioned the Monroe County Sheriff's office was hiring qualified deputies, and soon he was elected sheriff himself.

It was only a couple of months after he accepted the post that Natalie was found dead in the cove less than a mile from Rose Stone Cottage.

Grief over Natalie's death had morphed into anger and distrust of everyone around him. Slowly, he was overcoming the anger. A muted sadness, like a wound that never fully healed, remained, though. Their relationship had been fraught at the time of her death, and his inability to make amends left him perpetually guilty and remorseful. He hoped uncovering the truth of her death might ease the lingering pain, but being abandoned by his mother had taught him that some pain never went away.

Since Caldwell hadn't gotten along with any of his family since his mother had come looking for forgiveness he couldn't give, he had remained on Deadman's Cay alone after Natalie's death. He felt it would only make things worse to go home and answer their questions about why he couldn't accept her apology. With a prescription drug addiction, his mother had left Caldwell and his four brothers with their father when he was very young. She had cleaned herself up after leaving, but it had taken her years to work up the courage to ask her sons for forgiveness. By that time, the boys were all grown, and their father had passed away, leaving them to depend on each other. Caldwell's four brothers—Grayson, Beau, Briggs and Avery—hadn't understood why he couldn't let their mother back into his life.

The truth was, he was still trying to figure out how to let go of all the feelings of abandonment, loneliness and rejection that his mother's actions had caused. His intentions were to reconcile his relationship with his brothers, maybe even his mother, but he couldn't worry about that while islanders had suspicions that he might be involved in Natalie's death. Still, forgiveness seemed so much more urgent after losing someone…and losing the chance to make amends.

Caldwell's instincts told him those same suspicions were the reason Jayde had returned to Deadman's Cay.

Though he fully intended to confront her soon enough, Caldwell didn't want her to know he was following her yet, so he kept a discreet distance. He had seen her speaking to another woman as she left the dock, but they had parted ways after a brief conversation. Jayde had come alone. She went straight to the cottage, just as he had expected, located the spare key, deposited her bags inside the door and pulled Natalie's old yellow bike from the shed. It probably hadn't occurred to her that he lived there.

He wasn't sure why she left again right away, though. If she intended to go to the authorities, she was bound to be shocked to find him in charge. A few of the locals had protested his appointment as sheriff after Natalie's death, but outside investigators had cleared his name, leaving them unable to take any actions against him. But many still eyed him with suspicion.

Jayde and her family were among those that doubted his innocence.

As if Natalie's sudden death hadn't been traumatic enough for the family, Natalie's parents had also been killed less than a month later in a shocking automobile accident. The Farleys had been traveling on the mainland, somewhere near Atlanta, when the accident occurred. From what he heard, a semi had crossed the median on the interstate late one evening and hit them head-on. There had been no doubt that it had been an accident.

But Natalie's death had been different.

She had taken out the small watercraft they kept for personal use late one afternoon after Caldwell had been called to a crime scene, and she had never returned. Her body was found in a hidden cove on the southern edge of the island, washed up on the beach.

Investigators said Natalie had drowned and that it was a tragic accident, but Caldwell had never felt satisfied with that explanation. Natalie had been a strong swimmer and an experienced boater. Capsizing a deck boat on a calm, sunny afternoon and drowning in a shallow cove just didn't sound like a reasonable explanation for her death. Since investigators had ruled out foul play, he'd kept his suspicions to himself until he could dig a little deeper. He was sure they had missed something. She had been noticeably distracted by something in the weeks before her death.

Unfortunately, he had no idea what that something was.

What had bothered him the most was wondering why she had gone out in the boat alone in the first place. It wasn't something she normally did. Caldwell had questioned her mother and father, as well as a few close friends, but neither her parents nor friends had been able to fill in the blanks for him, making excuses that she was probably working on a new painting and wanted a different viewpoint. Whatever Natalie had been so obsessed with at the time was something she didn't seem to have shared with anyone else. He wasn't sure if that fact made him feel better or worse.

When he saw Jayde arriving on the island this morning, however, he had hoped maybe she might hold some answers, considering the cousins had once been close. That's why he was following her now. He just wasn't sure how to approach her yet. So he would have to be content to observe her actions for the time being.

He knew exactly when she began to get suspicious about being watched. She was starting to look around her as she approached the secluded cove on the gulf side of the island. The area was hidden from view by a stand of palm trees and buildings on one side and a low outcropping of rocks on the other. It was the cove where Natalie's body had been discovered.

What was Jayde looking for here?

She didn't look, however, she just put the kickstand down on the old yellow bicycle and, pushing her sunglasses onto the top of her head, settled herself on the sand looking out at the water. She sighed so deeply he could recognize the rise and fall of her shoulders from his place several yards away behind an old, deserted building on the edge of the beach. Jayde twisted and looked over her shoulder then and saw him peering at her from the corner of the stuccoed shop, and she glared back.

So much for his hope that she might not recognize him.

And since his cover, such as it was, had been blown,

he might as well approach her. She didn't move toward him or show any signs of being willing to cooperate with him, but he didn't care at the moment.

A pang of regret and loss hit him as the sun glinted off her deep auburn hair. The cousins had both inherited their grandmother's deep red hair, but that was where all similarity ended. Natalie had been shorter and willowy, where Jayde was tall and athletically built. The deep olive of Jayde's skin was an unexpected contrast to the deep auburn of her hair, while Natalie had been fair. Natalie's eyes had been a deep coffee brown. Jayde's were a vivid green, much like her name suggested. She turned them on him now as she scrambled to her feet, and it made him pause and suck in a breath.

"Stop right there, Caldwell Thorpe. I don't know why you've been following me, but I don't trust you in the least. If you come one step closer, I'll scream loud enough to bring the entire island running to my aid." Jayde held a hand out as she made the threat. She was also much more assertive than Natalie had ever been.

"Come on, Jayde. You know I'm not going to hurt you." Caldwell held up both hands to appear harmless.

"I certainly *don't* know that." She narrowed her green eyes at him and took a step back. Her disdainful expression slipped a fraction as she took in his uniform. "I thought you were an attorney. Why are you in a police uniform?"

Caldwell felt his jaw tighten. He didn't like the way Jayde's suspicion settled uncomfortably like a brick in the pit of his stomach. His middle churned with the discouragement that had often sucker punched him since being accused of Natalie's murder. He had experienced the ache, the nausea and the anger too much since Natalie's death. He had wanted to shout out that he wasn't guilty so many times but had to restrain his frustration. Getting angry would only make him appear more likely to have been involved.

But sometimes it was difficult to keep it in check.

He took a calming breath before speaking again. "I didn't kill her. I would never have done anything to hurt her. I loved Natalie. We had our problems like everyone, but there was nothing I wouldn't have done to work it out."

Jayde simply glared at him. "I have no reason to believe that. In fact, I'm going to figure out what really happened to her. I've already begun doing some research. This cove…where she was found. It has something to do with her death. Nat would never have capsized a boat and drowned. *Someone* intervened."

Caldwell had the very same suspicions, but he didn't know if now was the time to reveal that to Jayde. She clearly wasn't interested in his innocence at the moment. Instead, he decided to try to find out what she had uncovered so far. "What sort of research could you possibly have done? You just got here."

Jayde looked at the pearly white sand under her sandal-clad feet for a moment. "You can dig up plenty on the internet. You don't have to be in law enforcement to find clues. I think Natalie started believing the legend of Deadman's Cay. Maybe you did, too. Maybe she found something, and you wanted to get to the diamond first. But either way, I don't trust you enough to tell you what I know."

Caldwell had heard the legend, but he wasn't sure he believed it. More than one long-time resident of Deadman's Cay had mentioned the tale of a lost diamond hidden on the island by pirates. It was rumored to be a very rare pink diamond that had been stolen from a ship in the British Royal Navy back in the late 1600s. Discovered somewhere in Africa, it was bound for the British royal family with the intention of becoming a gift from King James II to his daughter as a wedding present. But pirates had heard of the Rose Stone and wanted the rare gem for themselves. After attacking the British Royal fleet, they had fled toward the Caribbean. The legend said they had been blown off course by a storm and run aground on Deadman's Cay in the Florida Keys.

According to the legend, the pirates had all died on the island, fighting among themselves for the last of provisions until they had slowly been extinguished. Hundreds of years later, the rumors of the Rose Stone's presence on the island were still circulating. Some even began to search for it. As far as Caldwell knew, no one could say for sure that it was ever found. It was said to guarantee loss and death for all those who touched it, thus the fighting and death among the pirates at Deadman's Cay, as well as the total loss of the British ship that had been carrying it to the king.

But in the early 1900s, a spyglass had been found in a cave along the beach, and a letter inside explained the existence of the gemstone. When historians began to research, they discovered more about the story. Later, the journal and ship logs were found as well, and placed in a museum.

There were some who argued that the Rose Stone itself had been documented in historical works, but he had never seen any of these documents. Most islanders outwardly scoffed at the idea that the stone was still hidden on the island, but Caldwell wondered how many secretly hoped to stumble upon the gem.

He had thought it was possible that the stone had been the source of Natalie's obsession. What he didn't know was *why* after all her years spent on the island. She had grown up vacationing regularly on Deadman's Cay and always seemed to ignore the legend. She'd said, many times, that the Rose Stone was just local folklore to attract tourists to the tiny island.

Natalie's parents had owned the island, and her grandfather before that. Everyone who lived here did so by renting or leasing from Natalie's family.

From me now, Caldwell thought, since ownership of the island had passed to him after Natalie's parents had died. It was still surreal. The only thing he didn't own on Deadman's Cay was a bit of public land that had been turned into a park and recreation area.

He wasn't sure why Jayde's parents or other relatives hadn't ended up with any of the property. He would ask her in time, if circumstances allowed.

For now, he needed to find a way to gain, if not her trust, at least her cooperation.

"Okay. I get that. You don't trust me. But this is my property you're on and the least you can do is be civil to me. Or you can leave." Caldwell decided to bluff. If she thought he had no intention of playing her games any longer, maybe she would relent. And right now he did have a job to do.

"I want you to know I fully intend to dispute that, as well. My aunt and uncle wouldn't have wanted you to end up with the island. Not after everything that happened." Jayde lifted her chin at him then.

He had started to turn away, so he half turned back to her and gave a shrug. "Fine. I really didn't want it. It just so happened to go to me. All I'm asking for now is some basic decency, Jayde. I'm still the elected sheriff."

"Convenient, isn't it?" Jayde stepped back once more.

"Think what you want about my involvement. My name has been cleared. I want to know what really happened to Natalie just as much as you do. But I have too much to do to stand here and argue with you."

Caldwell turned but had only taken two steps away from her when he heard her scream, accompanied by the pop of a gunshot.

He spun back toward her and dove to shield her body with his own. As they fell to the ground he registered a red smear across her left shoulder.

She was hit.

He carefully rolled her as they hit the sand, easing himself between the incoming bullets and her vulnerable form. One side of their surroundings was open water, and the horseshoe shaped cove was surrounded by trees and small buildings on the other three sides.

Caldwell helped her to her feet, urging her to stay low as he tugged her along toward the buildings. "We have to get out of here. This side of the cove is too visible."

She nodded jerkily, her face, damp from the humidity, draining to a pasty white. More shots ricocheted around them, and each time another shot sounded she flinched. He was thankful for his bulletproof vest as he shielded her as best he could with his own body and pulled her behind some rocks along the beach. There were too many cracks and jagged edges to offer much in the way of protection, however, and the incoming bullets sent bits of dislodged rock flying around them.

Jayde reached to cover her eyes to protect them from the spray of fine granite, but she let out a little squeak and dropped her arm again as the wound in her shoulder protested. Sweat was beading on her forehead from the humidity and Caldwell felt moisture collecting under his uniform, wishing for a nice fall breeze to ease the stifling air as he drew his own weapon, a Glock 17 service weapon.

The gunfire didn't slow as they hunkered behind what little shelter they had. He gripped the gun carefully with one hand, then used his radio to call for backup.

Dispatch promised help was on the way, and he focused on her once more.

Her breathing was loud, chest heaving a bit from the exertion as well as the adrenaline, no doubt. She raised her uninjured arm and swiped at her damp forehead.

Another bullet whizzed by too close. She cringed, leaning into him.

Jayde's breathing was becoming more rapid with every second. He had to get her out of here before she went into shock.

He looked around for any kind of shelter to keep them protected. He spotted a building along the edge of the beach that had once been a quaint café. It was deserted now, and the back door should be easy enough to kick in. It was on the side north of the cove and facing away from the incoming bullets. It was the best he could do for now. "There. See that building? Stay in front of me and run toward it as fast as you can when I say go. Don't hesitate."

She searched his face before nodding. "Okay."

Despite her previous spunk, her hands were shaking, he noticed, as she crouched beside him behind the narrow rocks.

He assessed their surroundings once more, squinting in the sun, which peeked out from the clouds once more. It had been threatening to brew up an afternoon storm all day, but it hadn't yet completely eradicated the bright island sun rays. After a thorough survey of the cove, he finally gave her the nod.

Jayde was fast, even with an injury, but Caldwell stayed right on her tail. On the side of the building shielded from the gunman, they paused at the old wooden door while Caldwell landed a well-placed kick to cave in the door lock. As it swung open, Jayde rushed in ahead of him. It was dark, damp and smelled of musty salt air. It was so stale she coughed, and he thought she might gag. Instead, she swayed with dizziness as the run and blood loss caught up to her. It took her a moment to steady herself.

Caldwell had drawn his Glock and pushed her behind him as he closed the door with his foot. He let go of her to call dispatch to see where his back up was, and groaned to find they were just getting his orders out.

"Caldwell?" Jayde's voice was weak behind him.

He was about to sign off with the dispatcher when he heard her sharp intake of breath just before she crumpled to the floor.

Before he could get to her side, though, a banging issued forth from the other side of the door.

The shooter?

Caldwell wasn't sure, so he couldn't focus on Jayde's wounds at the moment. Double checking to see that his gun was primed, he sidled up against the wall beside the door. If anyone came through it, he would get the drop on them first.

He glanced at Jayde slumped on the floor. It was torturous for him to just leave her lying there, but he wouldn't be able to help her if her attacker wounded or killed him, as well.

He had to focus.

Again, the pounding, and he knew it wasn't his backup, since dispatch had just reported their location.

In one swift move, he jumped, right foot first, at the door, swinging it open and aiming his Glock out the opening.

A grunt was his only response before the shooter

stumbled, tossed something with a gloved hand, and took off away from Caldwell's loaded weapon.

Caldwell shot into the air over his head, but the shooter ignored the warning and continued to flee. He aimed at the shooter then, but a scream from Jayde at the last second had him pulling up the nose of his pistol in surprise.

He turned to find her staring down a snake.

The shooter had fled because he had found another means of attack.

Caldwell didn't know when Jayde had awakened, but he was glad she had. "Don't move."

She was frozen with fear. A cottonmouth snake, still a little confused about how it got here, wound its way across the floor beside her.

"Is it poisonous?" Her face was clammy and pale now, the moisture of her sweat a fine layer on a pasty white background.

"Only if it bites you."

His poor attempt at a joke was lost on Jayde. She didn't let out a peep in response.

"As soon as it gets far enough away from you, I'll shoot it." Caldwell spoke in a reassuring tone this time.

Jayde whimpered as it came closer, just casually slithering up beside her, its tongue flicking in and out as it smelled its surroundings.

A cold shiver wended its way through Caldwell's form. He wasn't a fan of snakes, and cottonmouths were unpredictable.

Jayde's breath was coming fast once more, and the snake wasn't making any move to leave. He had to do something, and he couldn't shoot it with Jayde so close.

"When I say move, I want you to slowly go toward the door. If it follows, I'll get it. If not, I'll shoot it."

Caldwell's own adrenaline spiked, knowing what he would have to do.

If the snake tried to chase after Jayde, he would have to stop it, and the only thing he had available to capture it with was his bare hands.

But he wasn't about to let it bite Jayde.

He took a deep breath and watched as the snake began to slither closer to her. Pausing, it flicked its tongue a few times and went toward her.

"Now!"

Jayde took three huge strides to the door and the snake tried to follow. Closing his eyes for a split second with a prayer, Caldwell lunged for the snake.

He grasped it just as the huge white mouth opened toward him.

This is not going according to plan.

Jayde felt herself drifting in and out of consciousness as the thought came to her. She barely remembered where she was or what she was doing, but the fire in her shoulder served as an unpleasant reminder as an EMT prodded at the open wound. A shock blanket had been wrapped around her, as well.

She had been shot.

And then there had been a snake.

How Caldwell had managed to keep from getting bit, she didn't really know.

The last thing she remembered seeing before losing consciousness once more was the dark snake raised toward Caldwell with its snowy white mouth open wide while he reached toward it. How had he managed to wrangle it away from them both?

He seemed too good to be true, despite her first impression. It made her question everything.

And the shooter had set it upon her. She hadn't wasted any time making enemies, it seemed.

How had this happened? And with Caldwell Thorpe standing just a few feet away, proving he was not the one holding the gun.

Her investigation had already been full of surprises, for sure.

If he was really her cousin's killer, why was he trying to protect her from whomever was out to get her now? Was this some sort of setup designed to make her think they were on the same side?

She hated being so suspicious, but hadn't someone just tried to kill her? And hadn't her past experiences with men proven that she wasn't the best judge of character in that area? How did she really know she could trust Caldwell Thorpe?

She was going to have to try harder than usual to remember that with Caldwell Thorpe. Not only was he handsome, with his too long, wavy golden-brown hair and ridiculously blue eyes, but apparently also the heroic type. No wonder her cousin had fallen for this man. His broad shoulders and chiseled jaw were just the beginning of the attractions this man held for the opposite gender.

It wasn't as if she had gotten the details about his character from Natalie herself. Though they had been the best of friends growing up, Jayde had been estranged from her cousin at the time of Natalie's marriage. The cousins had grown apart after disputes over a variety of things, but mostly what Jayde felt was Natalie's failure to accept Jayde's relationship with Jayde's boyfriend at the time. Jayde later saw what Natalie had seen in the man, thus the distrust of men in general, but because of other disputes over family and such, they had only barely begun to make reparations to their friendship when Natalie had died.

She couldn't deny that this lack of closure had a great deal to do with what had brought her back to the island to find out what had truly happened to Natalie. If Caldwell was in any way involved, Jayde would find out.

She looked at Caldwell now, standing next to a deputy across the beach. He was watching the EMT work on her shoulder while he talked with the younger man, Caldwell's muscular form towering above them all, his intense blue eyes brooding and mysterious.

He filled out the forest green uniform he wore with a hard-earned physique. His strong arms extended below the short sleeves in tanned bulges. The bulletproof vest that hugged his midsection and chest did nothing but enhance the slim waist below where his gun sat snugly clipped into the holster.

His face was also tanned from the Florida sun, chiseled and masculine, and his hair reminded her a little of Keith Urban, the country singer. His scruffy beard looked unintentional, but not unattractive as it shadowed those strong bones of his face. The whiskers only made the blue of his eyes look brighter, in her opinion. No one should be allowed to have eyes that blue.

Those eyes drew her own with an irresistible force she couldn't put a name to. She wanted with everything in her to shake it, and yet she wanted to keep looking just as much. It was the most unsettling feeling she had ever felt.

He said something else to the young deputy beside him and then made his way over to where she sat on a gurney inside the back of the ambulance. She took a deep breath to steel herself against his nearness.

He didn't hold anything back. "So you came here to investigate Natalie's death. Someone else was just shooting at you, but you're convinced I'm somehow involved.

I think it's safe to say you weren't expecting this kind of greeting."

He gestured to her shoulder.

She sucked in a breath. "No, I definitely wasn't expecting to be shot. Like I said, I've looked at the facts from the investigation. I'm not satisfied that investigators followed up on every lead. I intend to find out why."

"Oh?" He raised a brow. "Well, I'm afraid playing Nancy Drew won't do any good. There isn't a single plausible lead that would indicate it wasn't an accident. I should know—I've done my own digging and I haven't found anything."

Was he just trying to find out what she knew? Jayde tried to cross her arms over her chest and winced as her shoulder throbbed. "Of course you haven't found anything. Why would you, if you killed her? And I'm sure you know how to cover up a murder."

He narrowed his eyes. "Did you not notice someone else was just shooting at you while I was trying to keep you alive?"

She didn't back down at all. "For all I know, you might have hired someone to shoot at me and make it look like you weren't involved. There are ways. Ways I've never even thought of."

"Yes, I suppose there are. I'll just have to prove to you I'm not involved. Tell me. What experience do you have at investigating murder?" He looked calm. Too calm.

She turned her eyes away from his. "What does that matter?"

"It matters a lot. How do you plan to find a killer? Do you know anything at all about collecting evidence? Who to call if you find something? How to protect yourself if someone else follows you? It looks like I might not have been the only one. Do you even know how long I followed you today?" Caldwell stepped closer.

"For a good while. Probably from the time I got onto the island." She shrugged, then winced at the renewed intensity of the pain in her shoulder.

"That's one right answer. And the rest?" Caldwell's voice had dropped to a near whisper and the soft, resonant timbre of his deep voice sent little shivers of awareness through her.

"I'll figure it out." She turned her face away.

"I'm not sure that strategy will work in a murder investigation." He chuckled.

She glared at him in return.

"What do you suggest? Working with you?" Her temper was flaring. The circumstances were beginning to annoy her greatly.

"No way. I don't need an inexperienced sleuth underfoot while I'm trying to figure this thing out." He was looking out across the island to where the beach began. The tide was beginning to change, and the turquoise waves were getting bigger. Darkening clouds on the horizon didn't bode well for the weather for the rest of the day. And the brewing turbulence mirrored her emotions.

"Maybe you should just let the professionals handle it." He finally turned back to look at her.

"Oh, yes. They did so well the first time." Her voice was full of sarcasm. She had reached her limit. She needed to be away from this man.

But she had to admit he had a point. She really knew nothing about conducting an investigation.

But that didn't mean she wanted to work with him any more than he wanted to work with her. He was getting under her skin. She found herself examining his face far more than she should, and her wayward thoughts often drifted to wondering what it would be like to have him comforting her in those well-muscled arms. How wonderful would it be to have him tenderly protecting and caring for her.

She shook off the warm, fuzzy feelings and tried to focus.

She was feeling the effects of the pain medication the EMT had administered to her, and her head felt a little fuzzy. Was that why she felt confused, or was she really starting to doubt Caldwell's involvement in Natalie's murder? But if he hadn't killed her, who had? Or had it truly been an accident like the outside investigators had asserted? Jayde struggled to focus her eyes and her thoughts.

What could have prompted the attack on her cousin? She had always thought she knew Natalie well, despite their temporary falling out. Was there something she was missing? Maybe Natalie hadn't been completely honest with her about everything. Things between their families had definitely made it hard to know how much they could trust each other, since the truth seemed to be something neither of their parents had told them.

Had Natalie been involved in something that had gotten her killed? Surely her cousin hadn't begun to believe in the legend of the Rose Stone.

She knew many islanders had heard the legend, but no one had actually been convinced of its truth well enough to try to find the treasure. It was really a ridiculous idea in Jayde's estimation. How could a rare and precious pink diamond have survived for this long in a populated area without being discovered?

"I don't have a lot of manpower on this island, but I'm going to assign a deputy to keep an eye on you until we can figure out why someone was shooting at you." Caldwell frowned over at the deputy he had been speaking to just before he walked over to the ambulance. "Ty O'Connor is a good guy, and he won't get in your way."

He turned to walk away, and Jayde was about to sink back in relief when he turned back to her with another question. "Where do you plan on staying?"

Jayde swallowed hard as it occurred to her that she might have inadvertently broken into Caldwell's home. She hadn't considered the fact that Caldwell might be living in the family cottage when she came. But of course he would be. Where else would he be living?

"I was going to stay at the cottage. Unless… You're living there, aren't you?"

Her eyes met his, and she knew his answer was going to complicate everything even more.

He nodded. "I am. But I can stay with a friend until you leave. I'll get the bicycle from the beach and put it back in the shed."

Jayde watched him go, mouth hanging open. Not only was he not going to tell her to leave, he was going to let her stay in the family's beach cottage while she investigated him?

His beach cottage.

He was pretty confident in one of two things, to be sure. One, either he knew he had covered his tracks so well that she couldn't prove him guilty. Or two…

He really hadn't killed Natalie.

And someone didn't want them to find out who had.

TWO

Caldwell couldn't believe what he had just done. He had just told Jayde she could stay at his house. She was here to accuse him of killing her cousin.

Perhaps her captivating green eyes had jumbled his senses.

Regardless of why, he couldn't take it back now. He had only one other place on Deadman's Cay to stay, and he would never live this down with his friend Parker when he asked. So after returning Natalie's bike to the shed, he walked across the island to the bungalow where his closest friend lived with his wife, Amelia. There was no point in calling first. He'd arrive on their porch before they could finish a phone conversation.

The Hensleys had lived on the island for the past five years, still childless but always trying for a family. Parker had been a lawyer for a short time, just like Caldwell, giving them that past career as common ground. Caldwell and Parker both had decided the life of a legal counselor wasn't what they wanted. Instead of continuing with law, Parker Hensley started a business on the nearby tourist island of Key West, where he and his wife commuted by boat a few days a week during the busier seasons. Their quaint restaurant and T-shirt shop kept them busy, and locals saw to it they had business year-round because of their excellent seafood.

Parker was sitting on his porch when Caldwell strode up the steps. He didn't look up from his phone right away, but spoke into the air between them.

"I heard family's in town." His voice sounded mildly amused.

"Not funny, Parker. You know why she's here." Caldwell snorted.

"Oh, we all know why she's here." He finally looked up.

Caldwell leaned against the porch rail. "I need a place to stay for a few days."

Parker guffawed at this. "You didn't. When she's here to point the finger at you? You think giving up your home for her is gonna change her mind?"

Amelia stuck her head out to see what the laughter was all about. "Oh, hey, Caldwell. Heard you have company."

This made Parker laugh all over again.

"News travels too fast on this tiny island." Caldwell shook his head.

"He let her have the cottage." Parker was grinning as he informed his wife of this juicy bit of news.

"What in the world…? Why did you do such a silly thing?" Her brow furrowed with incomprehension.

"I'm not sure. Just trying to be decent, I guess. Where else would she stay? Her home is in Atlanta with her parents. She doesn't really know anyone else here. According to Natalie, they stopped coming to the island years ago because of a family falling out. The siblings never got along after Natalie and Jayde's grandfather died. The Cambreys sold their beach house and never looked back." Caldwell pressed his lips into a thin line, his head swiveling from one of them to the other and back.

"How about Key West? Or maybe nowhere at all, and she can go back home. She's just going to dredge up bad memories for you by being on the island." Amelia's eyes filled with concern. She had become something of a sister to Caldwell in recent months, trying to mother him after Natalie's death.

"I understand where she's coming from, though, even if Natalie hadn't been my wife. They were cousins, and close when they were young. I'd want to be sure, too, if it was one of my brothers or something. I can't very well ask her to leave it alone when I have the same suspicions she does." Caldwell looked at the ground.

He knew the mention of his brothers wouldn't go unnoticed by Parker. His friend knew all about the Thorpe brothers and their differences. He knew Caldwell wanted to fix the rift, and he also knew that he hadn't yet made any real attempts to repair their relationships because he wanted to solve the mystery of Natalie's murder.

The twins, Beau and Briggs, had both tried to contact him when they heard about his wife's death. Grayson had come to see him. But things with Avery were still touchy, and Caldwell hadn't made much effort to restore a relationship with any of them yet, other than going to Beau's wedding a couple of months ago. When he arrived he had seen the futility of trying to repair the situation until he could put Natalie's unsolved murder behind him. He couldn't possibly put his full efforts into any relationship until he had reconciled the past. His emotions were still too raw.

"You know you're always welcome here. How long do you think she will stay?" Parker's voice had turned serious now, quiet even.

"I don't know. Longer than I would like, for sure. I'm not the only one who feels that way, though."

Caldwell told Parker and Amelia about someone shooting at Jayde earlier in the day.

"I wondered about all the excitement going on over on the far side of the island. I thought I heard gunfire. Parker was in the shower at the time." Amelia nodded. It was hard to miss anything that happened here.

Deadman's Cay wasn't much bigger than a small rural town, self-sufficient for the most part, but relying on the larger nearby island of Key West for many things. The islanders joked that you could stand on one side of the island and yell to someone on the other side, but it wasn't actually that small as far as land mass. The number of people living there, however, wasn't much. Unlike most tropical islands, many of the residents lived on large tracts of land surrounding their beachfront cottages and bungalows. The nearest neighbor was a decent jaunt down the oceanfront street for most residents. The middle of the island was made up of a few restaurants and shops, including a grocery store and some clothing boutiques. During the tourist season they catered to visitors, but throughout the year the stores focused on the needs of the locals.

Amelia pulled his attention back to the topic at hand.

"Who would be shooting at her? Do you think it's connected to Natalie's murder? Or do you think someone followed her here?" Amelia was watching him with her head at a tilt.

"It's more likely whoever shot at her was already here and even more concerned about her arrival than I am. She didn't mention any trouble before her arrival and it's a little strange that she was in the cove where Natalie's body was found when she came under attack, isn't it? It all just seems a little coincidental to me." Caldwell pushed away from the railing.

"Do you think she's going to be safe staying at the cottage alone?" Parker looked genuinely concerned.

"I have Ty keeping watch over the place. Hopefully that will be enough." Caldwell frowned up at the darkening clouds. They looked like they might open up anytime. "I'm going to go get my stuff out of the cottage and make sure she's settled in okay."

He thanked the Hensleys and started down the steps, hoping to beat the rain, but he could sense them exchanging a look behind him as he descended. He knew what they were probably thinking, and he agreed.

Jayde Cambrey had him acting completely out of character. He usually helped people within reason, sure. But he was going out of his way to assure not only her safely, but her comfort. Giving up his home went beyond making sure she had a place to stay.

Why he hadn't sent her packing was a mystery to everyone.

Jayde had no qualms about going back to the beachfront house her cousin's family had nicknamed Rose Stone Cottage and settling on the couch with a throw and a book to take her mind off her injury. If the throw's fabric smelled faintly of Caldwell Thorpe and the seaside cottage had little clues of his presence among the Farleys' old things, she ignored it all.

Evidence of Caldwell's character was dispersed throughout the room in the little things that had changed since he and Natalie had begun to live there. It still had a beachy feel, but the decor was now homier and more welcoming. Photos of Caldwell with Natalie made her chest ache, but there were also other family members smiling back from their frames. A couple of paintings that Jayde knew to be created by Natalie herself provided lovely accents to the room. Some medals hung on a wall next to a window, evidencing Caldwell's accomplishments in the line of duty. Heroic stuff. And all were recent. He couldn't be so bad, could he? A dirty cop wouldn't be awarded medals for selflessness and bravery, right? Her doubts about his involvement in Natalie's death grew.

She thought back to the early days after Natalie and Caldwell had married. She hadn't had much contact with Natalie then, but she remembered the remarks about him being an attorney. She couldn't recall being told about his change in career, and didn't understand how he could give up a potentially lucrative and noteworthy career to go into law enforcement, as he must have done shortly after their marriage. Two, three years ago? He had accomplished a lot in a short amount of time, it seemed.

She could also see Natalie's unique feminine touch all around her. Much of the decor was Natalie's taste. And Caldwell clearly hadn't changed anything since her death, assuring Jayde that he wasn't trying to erase reminders of her cousin. The shelf beside the window still held all her cousin's favorite classic novels in beautiful bindings, and Jayde reached for *Emma,* a lighthearted volume of Jane Austen's, instead of a collection of Sir Arthur Conan Doyle's stories of Sherlock Holmes.

She took the pain medication the EMT had suggested and settled in. Solving Natalie's murder would have to wait until the throbbing in her shoulder subsided.

It had taken her last bit of energy to get back to the cottage. Caldwell promised he would retrieve the yellow bicycle from the beach by the cove and return it to the shed behind the cottage. Deputy O'Connor took up his post nearby along the sidewalk. By the time she made it to the living room, grasping the book from the shelf and collapsing on the sofa had been all she could manage.

It finally started to rain, occasionally illuminating the cottage with flashes of lightning followed by low rumbles of thunder, and she was lulled into a comfortable stupor on the sofa while she became absorbed in the story.

Jayde read until she could no longer keep her eyes open and had just dozed off when a hesitant knocking sounded at the door. She thought she had imagined it at first, but then it came again a little louder. Before she could dislodge her legs from the lightweight blanket, the front door swung open.

Caldwell Thorpe stood in the door soaking wet, appearing almost frozen as their eyes met. "I, uh… Well, I need to get some of my things. I thought you might be asleep."

His awkwardness was endearing, the boyish uncertainty in his face making it obvious he was second-guessing his decision to come to the house. She considered trying to put him at ease but changed her mind, realizing she was feeling undeserved sympathy for him. It must have felt strange to him, knocking on his own door, though.

"I almost was." She sat up and folded the throw. When her eyes fell upon it, she found herself suddenly on the awkward end of the situation. It was most definitely Caldwell's, and not one left by her relatives as she had first assumed.

His eyes were also on the green and blue plaid blanket, but when she stood, he looked up at her face. "Sorry about that. I'll just get what I need and be gone."

She simply nodded, but before he could take three steps, he turned back to face her.

"Why was the door unlocked?" He seemed to have just realized it himself.

Jayde paled, realizing the severity of her mistake. "Was it? I thought I secured it when I came in."

He looked back toward the entry and shook his head. "Apparently not. I know you're injured and probably a little woozy from whatever medication the EMTs gave you, but you have to be more careful."

Anger suffused her form and she stiffened. "You don't think I know I should've locked the door? It was an honest mistake."

Caldwell changed course, stepping toward her. "I'm sure you do. But I have enough to do without having to look out for you while you're here. Do you think I want to get a call saying someone has attacked you again?"

"Maybe you do!" She could feel the anger beginning to shake her body. "How am I supposed to know you didn't intend to attack me yourself when you came in?"

"If you really believed that, would you be staying in my home?" Caldwell narrowed his eyes. "Surely you would know I have keys to the place."

He had a valid point. And the truth was, she really wasn't sure he could have killed Natalie. But what would happen if she let him know that? How would they go forward? They were enemies. The one time they had met after he had married Natalie, he had been giving her father legal advice about how to keep Jayde's boyfriend at the time, who had made a declaration that he wanted to buy her a ring soon, from getting any of the family's wealth.

Jayde had taken offense. None of them trusted her judgment and suspected her boyfriend of being with her for monetary gain. But she was also offended that her father had gone straight to Caldwell instead of speaking to her about it first. Caldwell had taken her father's side, claiming her father only wanted to protect her.

Jayde had felt that he only wanted to protect his money. Caldwell assured her that if her fiancé to be knew that the money wouldn't ever be his, it would prove his intentions were honorable and he was truly in love with her.

Caldwell and her father turned out to be right. Her boyfriend wouldn't agree to the stipulations Jayde's father asked and ended up breaking things off.

Jayde had never forgiven any of them for it.

She still didn't know how to read a person's intentions well enough to try another relationship.

What if her change of heart meant Caldwell would let her help him investigate? She didn't know if she could handle working that closely with Caldwell Thorpe.

She needed to stay as far away from his probing eyes and too-long, wild hair as possible. He reminded her of a pirate with his dashing good looks and dangerous smile.

But she wanted to stay close, even though she knew it wasn't wise. Some small part of her wanted to trust him and let him protect her. But she was afraid trusting him with her protection might lead to trusting him with her heart, because being near him made her feel tender things she didn't want to let herself feel. She had believed she could trust Dylan as well, and she had turned out to be wrong. She had believed his lies that he wanted to marry her, that they would be together forever… It turned out he wanted her family's wealth and someone naive enough not to know he was sneaking around with other women.

"Maybe it's best I just leave. I can find somewhere else to stay." She crossed her arms over her chest, not wanting her expression to soften, but feeling the anger seeping from her body despite her efforts. It was feeling more and more uncomfortable to be here in his home, especially with him standing here with her.

"No. I offered. Unless you're no longer comfortable staying here. I promise not to come in uninvited again while you're here. You should stay. I'll just get my things and get going." He moved toward the bedroom, and she stood transfixed. What now?

She looked around the room, unsure how to respond. "I'm going to get some dry clothes on."

Caldwell made his way down the hall. The ache in her shoulder was better, but she was drowsy from the medication. She sat back down on the edge of the sofa to get her bearings.

Caldwell came striding back down the hall to find her still sitting there on the cushion with the hand on her good arm resting against her temple. When she looked up, she could sense the tension still drawn taught in his demeanor. Her own form stiffened.

He moved into the room and sat down across from her. "Do you mind if I ask you a couple of things? It might help figure out some of the events from the day."

Jayde felt a knot pull tight in the middle of her abdomen. "What do you need to know?"

"Does anyone know, specifically, that you're here to look into Natalie's death?" His tone was gentle, unobtrusive. It surprised her, based on the apparently inaccurate perception she had formed of him.

She forced her thoughts to return to who would be shooting at her and why.

"I told my parents. Might've mentioned it to a woman on the ferry. We became friends pretty quickly. She seemed trustworthy." Jayde squeezed her eyes closed as the memory of the barrage of bullets hit her.

Caldwell thought back to seeing her speaking to the woman as she got off the ferry. He hadn't recognized the woman. But that didn't mean anything. The island was small, but there were tourists year-round. She could have been anyone.

"Could someone else have overheard? Someone standing nearby that you didn't really notice?"

"I suppose. There were a couple of other passengers." She opened her eyes, doubts filling them.

Caldwell didn't press any further. He had an idea she was regretting her honesty on the ferry enough already.

Before either could speak again, a knock at the door drew their attention from the problem hovering there between them. Caldwell's brooding blue eyes swung toward her.

"Are you expecting company?"

She raised a brow, gesturing around at the cottage where he lived. "Are you?"

Apparently not wanting to argue her point further, he went to open the front door. She didn't miss the hand on his holstered 9mm.

"Sir." It was the deputy he had called Ty O'Connor. "I saw you come in. I just found something, and I... Well, I think you should take a look."

A chill skittered down Jayde's spine. The deputy was young, and maybe inexperienced. But his body language was undeniable. His voice was low and serious. The rain running down the guttering sounded over the waves on the beach beyond, but it appeared to have slowed.

When Caldwell turned, likely planning to stay her with a command, she spoke before he had an opportunity.

"I'm coming, too." She was already slipping on her sandals.

He surprised her by nodding his acquiescence.

Ty led them down the wet sidewalk and around to the back of the cottage, where a roomy patio area graced the sloping lawn before it faded off down into the beach. There, stuck in the sand just where it took over the landscape was a shovel next to a large glass bottle half buried in the sand. Just beyond it was the real cause for horror. Natalie's old yellow vintage bicycle lay just beyond, mangled and smashed as if someone had run over it with a car.

The same bicycle Jayde had taken to the beach just before someone shot at her.

Someone was sending a nasty message.

"It was in the shed. I locked it up. I know I did." Caldwell gave Jayde a look that made her shiver. He stalked over to it, as if suspecting it might not really be the same bike. But it was.

She knew it carried memories of Natalie for him, because she herself remembered how Natalie had ridden it all over the island. Deadman's Cay, the island where practically no one drove a car.

"I suppose you could've made a mistake. I really thought I'd locked the door to the cottage, as well." Jayde stood rooted to the spot.

"No. I know I did. Look." Caldwell motioned for her to follow.

He dashed back up the slight slope to where the little shed stood at the side of the yard. She was panting a little when she caught up to him, more from adrenaline than exertion, but when she stopped before it, the lock was gone, and the door hung slightly ajar as if the wind had teased it partially closed. It didn't take much searching to locate the padlock, obviously sheared with bolt cutters, lying on the ground a few feet away. She was reaching for it when Caldwell called out a warning.

"Don't pick it up. There might be some prints." He was right there behind her as she looked toward the house only a few yards away. She had been so close to whoever had done this, right there in the living room of the cottage the whole time. Why hadn't she heard anything?

Without speaking to the two men, she dashed down to

the beach again. She took in the scene, wondering why this happened and what it meant, and then she froze, realizing the bottle had something inside.

Before she reached for it, though, she called out to Caldwell. "Can I touch the bottle? There's something inside."

"Wait a moment. Ty, do you have gloves?" Caldwell asked the question as he made his way back down the slope.

Ty loped over to his patrol car and pulled out a sealed bag with a pair of synthetic rubber gloves inside. Caldwell took them and pulled them on. He took the bottle from the sand before Jayde could protest and pulled out a rolled slip of paper.

It was typed in a weird font, that much Jayde could see from where she stood. Caldwell read it silently, face clouding with anger.

"What's it say?" Jayde nearly ripped it from his hands in impatience.

"It says, 'Some secrets should stay buried. Nosy redheads end up face down in the ocean.'" Caldwell closed his eyes.

Jayde couldn't hold back her squeak of fear. "Natalie's killer."

"It would seem so. He's been watching you." Caldwell looked around the property.

Ty cleared his throat. "Sir. Would you like me to take care of the evidence?"

Caldwell nodded. "Thank you, Ty. I'll keep watch over Miss Cambrey for a little while."

Jayde took a deep breath. "Shot at, threatened and it's only been a few hours since I arrived."

Caldwell eyed her. No doubt she was looking pretty pale at the moment. She should have been prepared for this. She couldn't deny it any longer. When she had first been shot at, she had wanted to assume they were only trying to frighten her away. But the threat was real. She had become a target.

"Come inside. I think we'd better get you out of plain sight." Caldwell was urging her toward the cottage as she tried to rein in her thoughts.

She allowed him to lead her into the house, and when she sat back down on the sofa, he disappeared into the kitchen for a moment. He returned holding two cans of Dr Pepper.

"I don't know what you like to drink, but this is all I have." He shrugged. "Or I can make some coffee if you'd rather."

She shook her head and held out a hand for the ice-cold drink he had pulled from the fridge. "This is fine."

He offered her a sheepish glance. "I drink way too many of these."

She attempted a smile. "It could be worse."

They fell silent as he settled in the chair across from her. Twin popping noises sounded loud in the silence as they both opened the cans. After a drink, he leaned back and sent a serious look around the room.

"I know you don't want to hear this, but maybe you should go home until I can figure this out. You aren't safe here right now." Caldwell's blue eyes settled on her face once more.

"I'm not leaving. It's too important to me to find out what really happened to Natalie. Besides, the killer might decide to follow me off the island." She took a sip of soda.

"I thought you might say something like that." Caldwell ran a hand through his wavy brown hair. "So you only have one other option. Working with me on this.

It's the only way I know you'll be safe. There's no way I'd let something happen to you, too."

Her pulse stalled and restarted at a more rapid pace. "You want me to work with you on figuring out who killed Natalie?"

He didn't even blink at her incredulous tone. "You knew Natalie like no one else. I know how to conduct a decent investigation. We both want to find her killer. It just makes sense."

"Except for the fact that we don't really even like each other," she retorted.

It was out of her mouth before she could stop it. "I mean—that's not what I meant, exactly. I..."

He surprised her by laughing. "It's okay. I know you kind of did. But I do like you, Jayde, whether you like me or not. That's irrelevant, though. We have a common goal. We can be adults long enough to do this for Natalie, right?"

He had the grace not to point out that he had been right about her ex-boyfriend.

A funny feeling in her stomach gave her pause. She knew he didn't mean anything by it when he said he liked her. Not like that, anyway. And he was right—she still had some antagonistic feelings toward him. If he was attractive, well, then, that was just too bad. A handsome face wasn't everything.

But he was right. They were adults. And she could do this.

For Natalie.

THREE

Jayde's emotions played across her expressive face. She seemed stunned by what he had said. Then she was uncertain about his proposal. But he knew she would relent when the determination had settled into her stubborn jaw. She had made a decision.

"Fine. We work together. For Natalie. But if at any time I feel like you're keeping things from me or I can't trust you, we go our separate ways." She spoke with her hands, he noticed. He found the habit endearing. She was an animated person, energetic and always active. He remembered Natalie telling him once that Jayde had been the athlete, while Natalie had been the artistic one.

At the pang of grief that hit him when he thought of his late wife, he stood and paced to the window. She had loved it here. She had always said it was her happy place. But even after they had decided to move here at the approval of her parents, where she could work on her art and be content, she had seemed distracted and distant. Things had just never quite been settled for her, though she tried to play the part of a happy wife for a long time.

Natalie had been prone to spells of melancholy that she had always laughed off as part of being an artist. Caldwell had disagreed and tried to get her to seek out some help, especially when she would get so down that she would hide out in the cottage for days on end. But she had waved away his concern and returned to her usual activities after a few days.

But whatever had overtaken her thoughts near the end of her life had become an obsession. He wasn't positive it had been the legend of the Rose Stone, but nothing else made sense. She had mentioned it in passing, but it didn't add up at the time. He had even begun to suspect she had met and fallen in love with someone else. It wasn't until after her death that he began to remember little snippets of conversations they had had mentioning the lost pink diamond. He hadn't thought she was truly starting to believe in it at the time. However, looking back, he realized how much she had been fixated on it.

"How much did you talk to Natalie before her death? What did she mention to you about the Rose Stone?" He stared out the window, allowing his thoughts to remain his focus as he asked the question. He knew if he looked at Jayde he would get distracted again.

"Not a lot, really. She asked me one day if I remembered hearing the tales about the diamond. Our grandfather used to laugh at us when we would ask about the legend of the Rose Stone, telling us it was just a fairy tale." Jayde's voice took on a nostalgic tone.

"She mentioned that to me, as well." Caldwell continued to watch islanders meandering around down the beach.

The ocean was several yards away, but there was little to obstruct his view all the way down the strip of sand extending out from his private beach behind the cottage and out to the public area on one side. His neighbors on the opposite side often frequented the beach during the day, and he assumed it was those neighbors walking down the beach now. His dock sat in the middle of the two parcels of land, and his personal boat was anchored there, bobbing alone and silent on the water. Tourist season had passed and those who inhabited Deadman's Cay year-round were the only souls left about. "Do you know of anyone else she might've talked to about the missing stone?"

Jayde remained silent for a few beats. He turned back to her as she spoke again. "Our other cousin, maybe. Tristan Vaughn is a nephew of my grandfather, Thurman Farley. Thurman is the grandfather I mentioned before. My mother had a sister and a brother."

"I don't think I've ever met this cousin." Caldwell felt a flicker of hope. Natalie hadn't mentioned speaking to a cousin about the legend. He only vaguely remembered Natalie mentioning having another cousin on the Farley side.

"Probably not. He lives on the mainland. I believe somewhere near Fort Lauderdale. I'm not sure where, exactly." Jayde squinted in concentration. "There isn't much of our family left, and Tristan has never had much to do with us. What little family we had wasn't close. My grandparents were both only children and none of their children had more than one child. I hate to say they weren't family oriented, but they just didn't seem to get along."

Caldwell had a feeling there was a reason they didn't get along, but it would likely come out eventually, so he left it alone.

"Do you know how to get in touch with him? Maybe he'll talk to us about what Natalie asked him…if she did speak to him." He watched her face and could see the doubt obscuring her expression.

"Maybe. We can try at least. He's a little… I guess you

might say he's a little standoffish. A successful business-man who doesn't like to waste his time." She seemed to be reaching for diplomacy.

"And I suppose he finds anything a waste of time if it doesn't include the opportunity to make money." Caldwell filled in the blanks. "Why would Natalie talk to him about the Rose Stone?"

"There was speculation among islanders that someone in our ancestry knew more about the stone than they were telling. But it was just rumors. Since our family owned most of the island, people were bound to say they had something to do with a missing treasure." Jayde frowned. "Especially since they had money."

"Missing? Or just never found?" Caldwell wasn't sure she had meant to say that. Was there a difference?

Jayde shrugged. "Some people said it went missing. Others said it was never found at all. It's all about as be-lievable as pirates burying a treasure here in the first place. I can't believe it wouldn't have ever been found."

"I see." Caldwell agreed with her.

"I'll think on what I've heard." Her expression clouded in thought. "Right now I think I'll find those pain re-lievers. This shoulder is throbbing so badly that I can't think straight."

Caldwell jumped to his feet. "I'll get it for you. Where did you leave it?"

She directed him to the kitchen counter and he went to retrieve the pills and some water.

He felt guilty for being so wrapped up in his thoughts that he had forgotten about her injury.

When he returned with the medicine and a glass of water, she thanked him.

After swallowing the pills, she set the glass on the table beside her. "I'll try to reach Tristan tomorrow and see if he can tell us anything. Is there anyone else we should talk to?"

Before Caldwell could answer, there was an odd noise at the rear door of the cottage, like a scraping after a thud. Their eyes met. "Maybe it's Ty. Stay put while I go check."

But a glance out the window revealed only clearing skies, and Ty's patrol car was gone. Caldwell pulled his Glock before peering out the window of the back door and slowly opening it. Only silence greeted him in the gathering dusk. The sinking sun cast odd shadows across the sloping yard. The memory of Natalie's mangled bicycle still mocked him from the beach just yards away.

He blew out a breath. Something had made the noise. Maybe a seagull or other animal, he reasoned. Closing the door, he returned to the front of the house to check that door, as well.

He had only taken two steps toward the living room, however, when the distinctive sound of a bullet piercing glass shattered the quiet.

"Jayde, get down!" He shouted the order, rushing into the living room.

She was already sliding to the floor to crouch beneath the large coffee table between the sofa and love seat. He hurried toward her, gun still drawn, and tried to get a read on the shooter's position.

Caldwell set himself like a shield between Jayde and the window. It wasn't long before another shot fired.

They ducked as low as they could as more glass splintered. He made a grab for his radio with his free hand to call for backup. Bad news met his ears.

"I hate to say it, sir, but it's going to be a while. There was a personal watercraft accident over near Key West and they've called out all available deputies." The kid working dispatch broke the news. It had been a while since they had a PW accident and usually only during the busiest part of tourist season.

"No one on reserve is still on the island?" Caldwell couldn't imagine what kind of Jet Ski wreck had needed every man available. It was mostly locals on the islands right now.

The dispatcher sounded eager to please. "I'll double-check, sir. But I think all the guys went to help."

In other words, the deputies were all bored and didn't want to miss some excitement since the tourists were gone.

Another shot hit the window. They were missing the excitement here, though.

At his and Jayde's expense.

Jayde stayed hunkered down behind Caldwell, grateful for his presence. She could hear the dispatcher's words, though, and didn't need to feel the tension radiating off Caldwell to know no one was coming. Not anytime soon, anyway.

She could only hope he had a backup plan.

"What now?" She swallowed hard and took a deep breath, struggling to control the rapid rising and falling of her chest. The house was too quiet aside from the un-predictable hail of bullets hitting now at odd intervals. They sounded closer with every shot.

"I'm going to try Parker. He'll come if he can. He knows how to handle a gun." Another shot punctuated his words.

Jayde flinched again at the sound. "Okay. What do we do until then?"

Her shaking voice belied the calm she was trying for. She certainly never had to face a situation like this working for an advertising firm in Atlanta. She had never even liked to watch police shows on television. She liked a nice, neatly ordered world where everything went as planned.

Being shot at twice in one day was definitely not part of her plan.

She had known looking for Natalie's killer would involve some risk, but she hadn't expected to become a target. She had also been surprised by the kindness she had found in Caldwell Thorpe, and she had no idea how to respond to the feelings it evoked.

"Just stay low and try to keep calm. I'm going to call Parker and then I'll see if I can get close enough to a window to see out. If I can see anyone, maybe I can wing him until backup can get here." Caldwell was already hitting the call button on his phone as he finished explaining.

She heard voice mail pick up on the other end and her hopes sank. "No answer?"

He shook his head as he began to leave an urgent message for Parker to come to the cottage as soon as he got the message. He didn't leave anything out of his voice mail—there was an active shooter outside the Farley cottage, he and Jayde had his service weapon to rely on, but nothing else, and no reinforcements were coming anytime soon from dispatch—to keep Parker from walking into danger unaware and disconnected.

Another shot glanced off the side of the house, and Jayde couldn't hold in a squeak.

She wasn't sure if their attacker was shooting out of frustration or what, but she wasn't about to give him something to aim at.

"Is he trying to hit someone or just terrorize us?" Jayde was frustrated herself, with the continued attacks.

"He seems to be trying to distract us." Caldwell listened for a moment. Shaking his head, he got his feet beneath him.

"I don't hear anything, but I'm going to try to get a look, in case he isn't alone. Stay here. Don't move unless I say so." Caldwell somehow made the order sound more caring than authoritative. Was it in her head?

She watched him move quickly across the room, ducking low the whole way and keeping his Glock carefully ready. He reached a curtained window and waited a moment before attempting a look. After another shot sounded he took advantage of the brief pause and leaned around to peer out.

"It's getting too dark to see." Caldwell ducked back down after a quick scan. "I'm going to try one more time."

When he did, he sucked in a deep breath. "He's coming toward the house."

"Can you get a shot at him?" Jayde didn't know much about shooting, but she knew the closer the guy outside got, the easier it would be for him to hit one of them.

His answer was to return fire. "I think I missed." Caldwell grunted in frustration.

He fell back below the cover of the wall, then crept over to another window. He caught her questioning look and explained. "Just in case he got a bead on where I shot from."

He reached the next window just after another shot fired and quickly took aim to return fire. This time a low yelp sounded outside.

Caldwell sent her a triumphant grin. "He was almost to the porch. I think I hit him in his shooting arm."

"Is he leaving?" Jayde didn't care that Caldwell had hit him as much as she just wanted him gone.

His expression sobered. Carefully peeking out the

window again, he grunted before slumping back down. "No. He's wrapping it up with something. I can't tell what."

He took aim and fired another round toward the shooter's apparent hiding place.

"Why won't he just leave?" Jayde hated the panic in her voice. The carpet scratched at her arms and legs where she huddled on the floor. The table and sofa on either side of her closed in on her, and she couldn't draw enough air into her lungs. She wanted to push them away but didn't dare. The agitation grew inside her, and she shook her head, trying to think of something besides the tight space. She could smell gunpowder, causing nausea to overwhelm her.

"Just hang tight. I'm going to try to incapacitate him this time." He sounded a little too happy about it, but was probably trying to keep her calm, she thought. She fought back an inappropriate giggle. What was wrong with her?

But before Caldwell could get up and fire another shot, rattling came at the door. Jayde was glad they had both checked and double checked to be sure it was locked behind them when they came in earlier. The villain was trying to force his way inside. Jayde's heart began to hammer against her ribs harder than ever before. Could he break in? What would happen if he did? She fought the ever-rising nausea as it swelled up into her throat. This was no time to make a break for the bathroom, and she would not embarrass herself by throwing up on Caldwell's floor.

"Jayde?" He was watching her, unconcerned with the hammering and kicking at the door. Why wasn't he worried about their attacker?

She swallowed hard, closed her eyes and willed the sickness away. She made a questioning noise in her throat to acknowledge his question, but her *hmm* came out weak.

"Are you okay?" He lowered weapon a little to examine her more closely.

She shook her head. "I feel sick."

Her eyes were still closed, but she could hear him stealing across the carpet in the quiet, and she realized it meant the hammering at the door had stopped.

Caldwell leaned in close and spoke to her. "Jayde?"

A sudden thud brought her eyes back open.

As the door came crashing open a terrifyingly large man with a gun rushed in.

FOUR

All the breath suddenly left Caldwell's body as a huge human form slammed into him.

The grip he had on his Glock loosened, and it fell from his hand and skittered under the coffee table. He had no time to waste in concern, however. Jayde's wide-eyed horror was replaced by a scream of terror as he lost sight of her. He recovered his balance and wrapped the man up in his grip, struggling to reach the SIG at the end of his right arm. Jayde had disappeared around the edge of the sofa, so he had nowhere definite to aim other than the sofa, where he couldn't see her exact location on the other side. Though he had a chance of hitting her anyway, Caldwell made sure he had to concentrate instead on dislodging him from his back before he could move very far. He writhed around the sizeable living room, knocking over lamps and tables as he went.

But Caldwell's grip was firm. He wasn't as agile, and every move he made was met with a quicker one by Caldwell. He tried to turn, and then attempted to flip him over his head, but Caldwell switched up his grip just in time to end up with the advantage. A bit too soon, however, he tried to grasp the gun with both hands.

A knee delivered a stunning blow to Caldwell's midsection, and he gasped for air once again. The large figure lumbered toward where Jayde had disappeared while Caldwell tried to recover. Caldwell attempted to call out a warning, but all he could manage was a hoarse gasp. The debilitating seizing of his lungs was taking far too long to lessen. He crawled toward them both.

Jayde said his name softly, no doubt testing his safety. He couldn't gasp out an answer, and unfortunately it gave the shooter a better idea of her whereabouts. He moved toward her with more stealth than his large frame seemed capable of.

But Jayde surprised them both by going on the offensive. She had managed to slip a very large conch shell from the bookshelf behind her while they were scuffling and, coming around the far end of the loveseat where it sat perpendicular to the sofa, she crept up behind him and brought it down hard on his head. It shattered and rained down over him on impact, temporarily stunning him enough for Caldwell to finally take action of his own.

He swept a foot out, knocking the SIG from his hand. It discharged, thankfully toward a wall of the cottage, before clattering to the floor, leaving a hole in the Sheetrock. He shook his head like a dog shaking off water and lunged toward the gun. Caldwell moved in before he could reach it, landing a hard blow to his unprotected jaw. It sent him reeling, and Caldwell kicked the SIG farther away from him.

The intruder roared in anger then and launched a beefy-fisted assault on Caldwell in return. Caldwell ducked most of his blows, but when a hard fist grazed his jaw, he stumbled back. Head still somewhat dazed, Caldwell swung hard at his opponent. The big guy swerved to the left, causing him to miss and lose his balance. He bounced a fist off the upper section of Caldwell's nose before he could duck the punch. He blinked rapidly, trying to clear his vision, but the shooting pain and tears pooling in his eyes made it next to impossible.

"Jayde!" Caldwell called out to warn her as his attention swung back in her direction.

Their attacker made for the SIG, but Jayde was faster. She snatched it out from under him and tried to get to her feet. His hand closed over her arm and yanked her toward him.

Caldwell lunged toward them, momentarily distracting him, but he didn't relinquish his hold on Jayde's arm. In a moment of quick thinking, she tossed the gun away as he pulled her to him, preventing him from using the gun to take her hostage. Unfortunately, however, it slid off in the opposite direction of Caldwell.

The intruder roared in fury and shoved Jayde away to make another move toward the discarded weapon. Caldwell dove at him again, this time knocking him off balance. By the time he recovered, Caldwell had snatched his gun and Jayde was pulling Caldwell's Glock out from under the coffee table.

Their attacker's face was mostly covered, but the eyes shrouded deep in the crevice of his face covering momentarily registered his defeat and fear just before he stumbled around the furniture and made for the door.

"Stop!" Caldwell called out, but despite the two 9mms that swung in his direction, he took his chances and bolted just as Caldwell pulled the trigger. He thought it grazed his leg, but he kept running.

Caldwell stumbled over furniture, trying to catch up with him but the perp was faster than he looked. Caldwell watched his form fade into the growing darkness. He didn't want to leave Jayde. There was no way of knowing if this man was working alone or not. Leaving her vulnerable was too big a risk.

Caldwell reluctantly returned to the living room. Jayde's hopeful expression fell.

"He got away?" She collapsed onto the overstuffed blue chair to her left when Caldwell nodded in confirmation. She sighed as if the last bit of her energy had left her body.

"I could have followed, but it was too risky to leave you." He looked down at the intruder's weapon still in his hand.

"Can you try to match the gun to the owner somehow? Shouldn't there be records?" Her voice shook slightly.

Caldwell made sure the safety was engaged before turning the SIG over in his hands. A blurred, scratched surface was all he found where the serial number should be.

"The serial number has been filed off. It's stolen." He frowned. "There's not much hope of tracing a stolen gun."

"You mean none at all." She rose and carefully handed his Glock back to him.

"Yeah, pretty much." He accepted his Glock and checked the safety before holstering it. "Are you okay?"

She simply nodded.

Her face was pale and the shock of what had just occurred seemed to be penetrating the fading adrenaline. "We *will* catch him, you know. I promise you we will."

He had stepped closer to her as he spoke, and for a split second, he thought she might allow him to comfort her. The thought of having a woman in his arms again was surprisingly appealing. But then her green eyes shuttered, and she turned away.

She wrapped her arms around herself, shivering slightly. "I hope it's soon."

* * *

It couldn't possibly be quick enough, in Jayde's opinion. She desperately needed away from Caldwell Thorpe.

Was it the danger she was in that was causing these emotions? She honestly hoped so. She needed an excuse to cling to, rather than accept that her heart could be so traitorous. The budding tenderness she was feeling for him surely stemmed from the gratitude she felt now that he'd saved her life—*twice*. He was a protector, a natural-born hero, and his actions didn't mean he was feeling any tenderness toward her. She had known he was a good guy before, despite their rough start. She just hadn't wanted to remind herself of his virtues because it lessened the likelihood that he had killed Natalie, and that left her with absolutely no idea who had.

But the one time she had met Caldwell before, she had seen it. He had been so protective of Natalie—so attentive. Despite her annoyance with his interference in her own affairs, she had been unable to deny Caldwell's devotion to caring for Natalie.

Jayde's mother, often trying to make things a competition between the cousins, had made an unflattering remark about Natalie's art. Caldwell had leaped to her defense, assuring them that Natalie was doing very well selling her paintings and had gained the notice of some influential people in the art world. Then later, Jayde's father's dog had rushed at Natalie outside. Sentinel was a large Rottweiler with an intimidating look and a gentle soul. But Caldwell hadn't known that. He had immediately put himself between Natalie and the dog and only relaxed when Natalie laughed and showed him how gentle Sentinel was. Sentinel had licked his hand in apology, and Caldwell had given Natalie a sheepish grin.

A man who went to that much effort for the woman he loved couldn't have killed her.

The pang of envy caught her unaware, and Jayde knew she had to find a distraction. She couldn't just stand here in Caldwell Thorpe's company thinking about how good he was.

"Do you mind if I look at some of Natalie's old things? Sketchbooks, paintings she was working on, things of that nature?" Jayde knew she didn't really have to ask, but she felt she owed him the courtesy.

"Of course not. You know where her studio is." Caldwell sent her a puzzled look, but he didn't question her. He muttered something about calling Parker back to let him know the man was gone. She wasn't sure her attacker wouldn't return. She wanted to ask, but his actions changed her mind.

She heard him leaving a message as she went up the stairs. She thought he might follow her, but he turned and strode back out onto the porch instead. Maybe he was going to keep a lookout for any other strange behavior.

She knew it was difficult for him not to go after the guy, but he wouldn't leave her alone right now. So she would just have to occupy herself while he was completing reports and speaking with the deputies about finding their attacker.

Jayde climbed the narrow staircase to the studio upstairs which overlooked the island on one side and the ocean on the other. The room stretched across the whole top of the cottage.

The cottage was a typical island home, a squat two story Craftsman, but it had some coastal elements to its square shape. The upper story was comprised of dormers that extended in the front but squared off in the back. It had once held two bedrooms and a full bath along one wall of the home, but now only columns marked the places where dividing walls once stood between the bedrooms. Windows on three sides allowed plenty of island light to pour into the room, and the positioning of the easels promised Natalie had made good use of it.

The outside of the cottage revealed the raised foundation to accommodate flooding beneath an aqua blue siding trimmed in white. The typical large island porch held bloom-filled flower boxes all the way around its railing, and white wicker rockers sat on either end. Large planters scattered around the porch also held flowers in many riotous colors and filled in with lush greenery. It had a cobbled drive but sat surrounded by sand all the way around its deck and porch.

But inside, as she came to the top of the lacquered wooden staircase, it opened into the light-saturated room. Art supplies were discarded almost comically over every available surface. Jayde could practically imagine the smell of her cousin's floral perfume mixed with the paint and stripping chemicals. In her mind, she could see Natalie at work, standing before one of her easels, biting one side of her lip as she applied the brush delicately to her canvas.

Her cousin had approached her work with joy, but it was sporadic. Natalie had struggled with ups and downs in her mental health. When she was down, her motivation to paint often waned. Jayde couldn't help wondering how Natalie's mood swings had affected Caldwell. Had he responded with patience or frustration? Jayde had often felt frustrated with Natalie herself when they were younger and her cousin didn't want to play because she didn't feel well. As they had grown older, Jayde had started to understand, and Natalie had developed ways to cope with the highs and lows. One of the ways Natalie had dealt with the emotions was by learning new things, or completely focusing on something she was very interested in. Some had called the behavior obsessive, but Jayde understood Natalie had needed something to immerse herself in. It grounded her.

Sometimes Jayde felt the same way. Like now, when she was fighting to overcome her grief over her cousin's loss. She knew her determination to find Natalie's killer also fulfilled her need to keep her own mind occupied.

But in moments like this, the sadness of losing Natalie overwhelmed her motivation to keep up with her investigation.

Tears welled in her eyes, and the ache in her chest swelled in her throat. She really had to stop thinking about losing Natalie and get to work on a resolution.

She meandered through the room, picking up a paintbrush here and a drawing there. Curious about her cousin's work, she picked up a sketchbook and began to thumb through it. Natalie had been very good with detail and people, so Jayde wasn't surprised to find many of the pages filled with beachgoers at play in the still-lifes she had created. In some they simply interacted on the sand along the shore, but in others, unfamiliar faces smiled back at Jayde. A few were from visits to Key West where Natalie had often gone to promote her work among tourists.

Jayde was about to return downstairs when a landscape caught her attention.

It wasn't easily recognizable at first because Natalie had drawn the shoreline and the rocks close-up, but the steps created by the rocks where the water had eroded away their surfaces above the waterline were familiar. They led up to a small cave.

It was from the cove where Natalie's body had been discovered.

Was it simply a coincidence?

Jayde looked through the rest of the sketchbook but found nothing else that seemed significant. Maybe Natalie had simply found the cove beautiful and a good subject for a drawing. *Probably nothing more than a coincidence.*

Jayde flipped the book closed and returned it to the drawer. She sighed, realizing she might never know the truth about the landscape drawing.

She looked around the room a little more, but it wasn't long before her sadness became oppressive. She started down the stairs when she ran into Caldwell coming up.

"I was coming to tell you I'm going to head out if you're okay. Ty's back on duty for the next few hours, so you won't be alone." Caldwell stuck his hands in his pockets. "I'm gonna catch a nap while he's here so I can stay on the lookout this evening. I've been on watch, and the gunman is long gone. I doubt he'll come back tonight. He knows we may expect him to, and we'll be ready if he does."

Jayde made a noise of agreement. Her stomach turned over at the thought of another incident like the one they had just experienced, but she knew she couldn't live in fear. Life had to go on. "I'm going to try to call Tristan. If Natalie spoke to him, maybe he can give us some sort of lead."

He followed her stare out the window along the stairs. "Good idea. I never met him, so I doubt he would give me much information."

"Maybe not. Do you want to wait while I call?" She gestured toward her phone. "I doubt I'll get to speak with him right away, but I can try."

Caldwell hesitated. "It might help, if he does answer."

Jayde nodded and tried the call. After a few rings, a

woman's voice answered. "Oh, I'm sorry. I was trying to reach Tristan Vaughn. Is this still the correct number?"

She paused and listened as the woman confirmed that it was his office contact number, and he was currently out of town.

"I see. Does he have another number where I could reach him? I'm his cousin and it's a family matter." Jayde used her most polite tone. She pulled the receiver away from her ear to put it on speaker, ostensibly to take down the number.

Instead the woman snapped out a reply. "I don't give out his personal number. If you're close enough to him to be bothering him, you'd already have his information."

With a rude click, she disconnected the call.

"Well. That went about as expected. Maybe Natalie did try to contact him. That woman seemed to have some experience with that kind of call." Jayde's face flushed with irritation at the woman's brusque manner.

"Don't worry about it. He probably didn't know anything, anyway. If Natalie received the same response, he's likely never spoken to her." Caldwell winced.

"I suppose you're right. It was worth a try." Jayde set the phone down beside a jar of paintbrushes. "Is there anything else I can do while you're gone?"

"Not at the moment. Probably best to lie low for the rest of the night. I'll be back before ten." Caldwell tipped his head in her direction and turned to go.

"Caldwell?" Jayde felt almost uncomfortable saying his first name. "Er, Sheriff Thorpe."

"Caldwell is fine." Their gazes collided as he swung back around to face her.

"It's painful, I know, but… You've gone through all of Natalie's things, haven't you?" Jayde laughed nervously. "That's probably a silly question."

"No, it isn't. I've started going through some of it. I probably wouldn't have if I hadn't been looking for clues. Not yet, anyway." He winced slightly. "It *is* painful."

Jayde looked away.

"Are you okay?" His gentle query came unexpectedly. He seemed genuinely concerned.

"Yes. As 'okay' as I can be in this situation, anyway."

He nodded. "I understand. Is there anything I can bring back for you? Something to eat?"

Jayde swallowed. "I'm not really hungry. But thank you. I can scrape up something from the kitchen if you don't mind."

Caldwell looked her over for a long moment. "No, I don't mind. I'd definitely feel better if you ate something. If you change your mind, call me. I left my number in the kitchen. If you need anything at all, call or text."

After Caldwell left, Jayde double-checked the locks before making some iced tea from the tea bags she found in his kitchen and settling once more in the overstuffed blue chair. Her shoulder was still throbbing, and she had little of interest to her there to distract her. She didn't usually watch much TV and games didn't sound appealing right now. Her mind would be too busy trying to riddle out what had happened to Natalie to attempt to read again. After all, that was why she was here, so why not try to find something?

Jayde rose from the chair and headed for the downstairs guest bedroom. She remembered Natalie confiding to her that she hoped to make it into a nursery within the next few years. Thoughts of Caldwell as a father made her anxious to dismiss the memory. No doubt he would have been a good one, but envy made her uncomfortable and that's exactly what she felt at the idea of Caldwell raising another woman's child.

Shame and guilt flooded her. How could she be having such thoughts about her late cousin's husband?

She threw herself into her search. She went to the closet and began going through storage boxes. Jayde and Natalie had stayed in this room during vacations when they were young girls. The families had all come together only once after the big argument about which Natalie and Jayde were never privy to the details. The adults had seemed distracted, not wanting to be bothered with the children. They tended to focus more on business and social connections in Jayde's memories.

Back then, the art studio had been two attic bedrooms with a full bath between them. Natalie and Caldwell had remodeled the upstairs after they came here to live, making the two smaller attic bedrooms into Natalie's art studio. This room, however, still housed the queen-size bed from their childhood and many of the boxes were simply filled with old pictures and decor from when Rose Stone Cottage had been only a vacation home.

By the time Jayde had gone through all the boxes in the lower half of the closet, she had decided she wasn't going to find anything useful. But with nothing else to do, she decided to go through the things on the top shelf, anyway. But she would need a stepladder to reach them.

Jayde knew the stepladder was probably in the shed, but it would only take a few minutes to go out and get it. She could easily be safely back inside the house before anyone realized she had left.

Using the flashlight on her phone, she hurried out to the backyard, shuddering, despite the heavy, humid air, at the memory of the bicycle's fate. She refused to be frightened away so easily. It only took a few seconds to find the stepladder, and she shoved her phone into her pocket to free up her good hand to grab it.

She dashed back to the house as quickly as she could with her awkward armful, breathing a sigh of relief as she reached the back door and locked it behind her. She scanned the room, but nothing was different. Everything was as she had left it.

Back in the closet, she settled the stepladder in place to pull the boxes from the shelf. When she tugged at the first box, however, she lost her balance. She released the box to grab hold of something to steady herself with her good arm, but the first thing her hand found was the clothing rack. Her unsteady weight loosened the bar just as the box she had released tipped forward onto her head. She threw her uninjured arm up to protect her head as the shelf, boxes and all, came crashing down as the bar beneath it pulled away from the wall.

The last thing that registered in Jayde's mind before blackness took over was a gaping hole in the side of the closet.

FIVE

Caldwell's mind wouldn't shut off, and he was still struggling to get some actual rest when his cell phone began to ring. He rose reluctantly to answer, but as soon as he saw it was Ty, he was fully alert.

"Sir, I heard a crash in the house. Miss Cambrey didn't answer the door when I knocked, so I peeked in the best I could, and it appears she's fallen in one of the bedrooms. The light was on but all I could make out through the curtains was a pile of boxes. She isn't coming to the door when I knock. I'm afraid they might have fallen on her." Ty reported the news from the other end.

The young man had only been on the job for a couple of months, and though he was still learning a lot, he had good instincts. He still got excited over any action, though. Caldwell remembered well how the adrenaline once spiked his heartrate when there was danger on the job.

"I'm on my way. There's a key beneath the flowerpot on the west side of the porch. Go on in and check on her." Caldwell disconnected and went to find his boots, hoping Ty might be overreacting a bit.

He arrived to find Ty crouching near Jayde in the guest room downstairs, trying to unbury her. She was stirring, but not fully awake. She was near the middle of the bedroom, and it looked like the entire closet had come crashing down on her.

He reached her side about the time her eyes popped open, and she began to struggle against the remaining pile of boxes pinning her to the floor. He cautioned her to remain still and let him move the debris.

"Caldwell, I'm so sorry. I just lost my balance and grabbed for something." Her words were rushed and came out a little mumbled, but he understood her.

"It's okay. They're only boxes. Easily put back in the closet." He began lifting them off her.

"No, Caldwell, not just the boxes. *Look*." She jerked up and pointed wildly at the closet.

He leaned inside at her urging and found the reason for her upset. The Sheetrock was fractured and pulled loose off the wall where the bar for hanging clothes had been torn free. A gaping hole remained. But the hole wasn't what fascinated him. One edge of the damaged Sheetrock had torn away in a perfect line. The seam was tucked into the back of the closet near the corner and the edge looked different.

Jayde began to struggle once again, drawing him out of his stupor. He helped her finish moving the boxes, then he pointed at the closet.

"There's something odd about this wall." He motioned for her to come look.

"Why did it break like that? So straight along that one edge?" Jayde tilted her head as she examined it.

"It looks like there's something built into the wall. A hidden panel or something. That's probably why the clothing rack was so unstable. It's a wonder it's held on this long." Caldwell moved in front of her and began moving his hands along the edge of it. He pushed on it a couple of times also. "There must be a release for it somewhere but I'm not finding a catch."

"Maybe it's somewhere else. I mean, to disguise it as part of the wall, it wouldn't necessarily be accessible from here." She was watching as he pressed against every edge.

"Okay, fair enough. Where else would it be?" He stopped pushing against the wall.

Jayde looked around. "Not too far away. If you wanted to keep everyone from knowing about it, you'd need to be able to see the door when you tripped it."

Caldwell followed her eyes around the room. True, he had found Natalie coming out of this room a time or two when she was alive. He had assumed she had been in here daydreaming about babies and nurseries. If she had found something here, why hadn't she told him?

A deep sense of betrayal stabbed at his chest. He couldn't do this right now. He turned to leave the room. Jayde was fine, save a couple of bumps and bruises. And finding a hidey-hole in the closet wouldn't bring Natalie back.

What if they found something he didn't want to see?

He had only vaguely suspected Natalie of being unfaithful to him before, but what if she had actually been involved with someone else? What if he discovered she hadn't been who he thought she was? There was no telling what kind of secrets she might have hidden from him.

"Where're you going?" Jayde called from behind him.

He couldn't answer her. He didn't know where he could go to escape the memories. Hadn't he just told Jayde he was determined to find Natalie's killer? And now he was breaking down over the possibility of finding one single clue. He had no idea how to explain to her something he couldn't even understand himself. He had to toughen up. His brothers had told him more than once that he was too sensitive. And if he wanted so badly to figure this out, shouldn't he be wanting to latch on to anything he could find that might lead him in the right direction?

Caldwell kept walking until he reached the back door. He went right past Ty, ignoring the confused look the deputy gave him. When he reached the cool sand, he sank down on it in the cool night and put his head in his hands, not caring if others could see him.

How had he let her down so badly? He felt so unworthy of her right now. So unworthy to be the one still living when Natalie had been so much better than him in every way. She had been loving and generous. She was the first to donate art for benefits and charities. She had worked in the nursery at church, taught teens how to paint and did whatever needed doing for the elderly around the island, from weeding flower beds to bringing the occasional dish to a church function. She had been a peacemaker among her friends.

Caldwell had done none of those types of things. His excuse had been that working as sheriff was public service in itself. He didn't like advising anyone, and he certainly hadn't been afraid of confrontation.

He felt selfish now.

The soft sounds of bare feet sinking through the sand behind him alerted him to Jayde's presence a few minutes later. She didn't speak, she just sat down beside him and watched the waves coming in to shore in the moonlight.

"I'm afraid to learn what she was hiding from me. I already know she was hiding *something,* and that's painful enough."

He wasn't sure what made him want to confess this to Jayde, but it felt right.

Jayde sighed. "Natalie loved you. If she hid something from you, I know she must've had a very good reason for it."

"We were always open and honest about everything. At least I thought we were until recently. So my thoughts go to the worst possible scenario." He pushed back the lock of slightly wavy hair that was falling over his forehead.

Jayde sat up a little straighter. "I hope you don't mean to tell me that you think Natalie was having an affair. Because we both know she would never do that."

"Do we? What if I really didn't know her at all?" Caldwell almost choked on the words when Jayde's soft hand came to rest on top of his own.

"I can't believe you would even consider that. Are you sure you aren't the one who just got hit in the head?" Jayde laughed.

"I'm sorry about that. Are you sure you're okay?" He gave in to a smile, but he was looking closely at her for signs of injury. It was thoughtless of him to be so worried about himself when she had just suffered a blow to the head hard enough to knock her out, with her shoulder still wounded, as well.

"I'm fine." Jayde rose and offered her hand to him. "Come on. I think I know where we can find that latch."

"What?" He took her hand, but she didn't answer until they reached the guest room.

"Look." She pointed at the wainscoting along the wall adjacent to the closet. "There's a small seam there. I bet if we feel around on it we can find a place that will open."

"You think it opens on the outside rather than in the closet?" Caldwell walked over to the wall for a closer look.

"Mmm-hmm. I think the seam inside the closet is

just where the back of the hidden panel rests. I climbed in there and looked at the edge with my flashlight. It's sealed off back there." Jayde leaned in beside him and began to feel along the trim on the top edge of the wainscoting.

She sucked in a breath just before he heard a faint click and a crack appeared. Caldwell could barely grasp it with his fingertips, but he managed to ease it open.

"A book?" Jayde looked disappointed.

"Did you expect to find the pink diamond?" Caldwell teased her. "I thought you didn't believe that legend."

She groaned. "I don't. But this looks new. It isn't interesting at all."

"I'd say that depends on what's inside it." Caldwell pulled the book out and flipped it open.

Natalie's neat script stared back at him from the pages of the leather-bound journal, bringing back memories he'd rather not recall.

Jayde must have recognized Natalie's handwriting, as well. She sucked in a breath. "I wonder what she was writing about that she felt the need to hide."

He wondered the same thing.

Bracing himself, Caldwell flipped to the front page of the journal and found an opening sentence that sent him reeling.

I can't believe I'm about to write this, but the Rose Stone is real.

Jayde couldn't hold back an incredulous laugh. She knew Caldwell had read the words, as well, for he was stiff and motionless beside her.

"I don't believe it. This must be some kind of trick. Natalie would never have believed the Rose Stone actually existed." Caldwell was now shaking his head in denial.

"A trick? That's unlikely. What reason would she have had to trick us? And what would that have to do with her death?" Jayde stretched out a hand for the journal.

Caldwell handed it over, eyes narrowing. "I don't know. But it can't be true."

Jayde lowered into a chair near the closet and began to read the next line aloud. "'My husband would never believe me. I doubt anyone will until I find the stone. But I'm getting closer as the hours go by. Today I found a crude map tucked into that ancient-looking spyglass Grandfather kept in his office.'"

Caldwell was still shaking his head.

Jayde paused to explain. "Grandfather left it to Natalie when he died. She was always fascinated with it."

"I remember it." Caldwell gestured to the journal. "What else does she say?"

Jayde cleared her throat. "'I believe it to be one of at least two pieces of the puzzle he left us. Either Jayde or Tristan may have the rest.'" She paused to look up. "What could she mean?"

Caldwell shrugged. "Did your grandfather leave you anything when he died?"

Jayde pressed a finger to her lips as her mind worked. "Just a fancy old pocket watch. Nothing would fit inside it, even if it comes apart. I've never tried to take it apart."

"Do you happen to have it with you?" Caldwell gave her a hopeful look.

"Sorry, but no. I tried to pack light for this little adventure." She couldn't hold back a smile.

"I figured as much. Is there anything else there?" He was looking at the journal again.

Jayde scanned the page, but the rest was just speculation on her grandfather's intent. She turned the page. "Here."

Jayde laid a finger on a line near the top. "'I'm going to hide the map with the spyglass and the ship's logs and compass in the attic. But I know where to look now, and I'm going to find it.'"

"The attic here? I didn't know there was an accessible attic. Do you mean the art studio?" Caldwell was looking uncomfortable now.

Jayde couldn't blame him. She felt a bit betrayed that Natalie hadn't confided in them herself.

"The attic itself is actually through the back of the linen closet in the upstairs bathroom. You didn't remodel the bathroom, did you?" Jayde asked.

He shook his head. "No. But why she never felt the need to tell me it was there I don't know. Why wouldn't she trust me with this?"

Jayde felt a pang of regret for him. It had to hurt, facing the fact that Natalie had kept secrets from him. But she had kept secrets from Jayde, too. They had once been best friends. Jayde had known Natalie far longer than Caldwell had. It seemed likely that she would have confided in Jayde, too.

"I don't know, but maybe we can find out." The hurt seeped into her voice, and she let it. He might as well know he wasn't alone in his feelings of betrayal.

"Before we go check out this secret attic, does she say anything else we need to know?" Caldwell didn't look her in the eye. She didn't focus too deeply on his reasons.

Before she could answer, though, Ty rapped on the door frame. "I'm sorry to interrupt, Sheriff, but Andrew's here and wants to talk to you."

"Tell him I'll be right there." Caldwell waited until Ty

was gone to speak again. "Put it back in the wall panel. We'll come back to it later."

Jayde ran a hand over the cover of the journal she had just closed. "Okay. Who's Andrew?"

"He's another deputy. Andrew Siebert. His father, John, was the sheriff a while back." Caldwell didn't say any more, but Jayde got the feeling the two men weren't the best of friends.

"I remember Sheriff Siebert. From a long line of pirates, we used to joke." Jayde's lips curled faintly at the memory. "Long John Siebert?"

Caldwell smiled in one corner of his mouth. Maybe he could see the humor in their nickname for the old sheriff. Sheriff Siebert had worn a long silver beard and kept his hair longer than most men on the force, as well. She could easily picture him with an eye patch or peg leg.

He shook off the thought. "Wait here, okay?"

He disappeared, closing the door behind him. Jayde thought the action a little bit odd, but she returned Natalie's journal to its hiding place and settled back into the chair to wait for Caldwell to return.

A few minutes later, she realized she could hear bits and pieces of what the men were talking about, especially when they began to raise their voices. She hadn't meant to eavesdrop, but when she heard the bicycle mentioned, her curiosity won out.

"...know it was probably some kids playing a prank." It was an unfamiliar male voice. Andrew Siebert? It must be.

"...not just a kid." It was Caldwell this time and he sounded angry. "You need to do your job, Deputy Siebert."

"You're paranoid. You just can't accept it was an accident." Siebert spoke again. Silence filled the cottage for a long moment. Jayde had no doubt at all that Siebert wasn't referring to the recent incident with the bicycle.

"Get back to your patrol, Deputy." It was cold and left no room for argument. She also had no doubt Caldwell was furious in that moment.

Jayde couldn't hide her heated face when Caldwell came back into the room.

"I guess you heard our conversation?" One eyebrow elevated into his wayward lock of hair that always fell over his forehead. His face was still flushed with anger.

"Only a few words. But enough. I didn't mean to. But when I thought I heard you mention the—the bicycle…" Her words trailed off as she stood and wrapped her arms tightly around herself.

"He botched the investigation, is what it boils down to. He tried to blame Ty, but I know Ty followed procedure, because I watched him. I didn't let Andrew know that, though. He's hiding something." His anger had only faded slightly.

"You don't care much for him, do you?" Jayde asked carefully.

He turned his attention back toward the open door he had just come through. "He's never given me any reason to dislike him. It's just more of a gut feeling. He's not done anything shady that I know of, but sometimes I see something I don't like in his character."

"Like what?" Jayde stepped closer to him.

He half turned to see her face. "I don't know, like kicking a dog when he gets impatient, or ignoring a friendly kid when he knows they look up to law enforcement. Just things that make me question his true integrity."

Jayde nodded. "I would, too. It's a small man who mistreats kids and dogs, in my opinion."

He turned back to her. "I need to go to the main station. It seems we have an officer missing. His partner says they were separated trying to apprehend an armed robber and he never found him. He isn't answering his radio. They need everyone available to help locate him. Would you be okay going with me? I'd feel better about your safety since I won't be here on the island."

"Okay. Where is this station, exactly?" She tried to keep the weariness from her voice, but it had been a long day.

"Key West. It's the county seat of Monroe County. We'll have to go by boat." He seemed to think this might deter her.

It didn't. She was actually ready to get away from Deadman's Cay for a little bit, even if she was exhausted. "Okay. I'm ready when you are."

His face relaxed. "Good. Then let's go."

It was only a short walk to the docks where Caldwell's county-issue watercraft waited. Jayde half expected another attack as soon as they left the house, but Caldwell was quick to reassure her it was safe.

"I have Ty and my good friend Parker Hensley both keeping watch. If he's gutsy enough to try again right now we'll catch him. I suspect he will lay low for a bit."

The boat was a simple watercraft, and Caldwell handed her a plain orange county-issued life vest to put on before indicating the bench beside him for her to sit on.

"It isn't too far to Key West. I assume you came over on the ferry from the mainland?" He checked her life vest before moving behind the wheel. He didn't sit but planted his feet so he could better see what was ahead in the dark. A large light that reminded her of a spotlight was the only means of illumination in the black sea.

"Yes. But I've been across to Key West before. It's just been a very long time." She felt awkward perched on the bench beside him, but he was focused on steering the boat.

"This boat will be faster than the ferry."

The waters of the Gulf were choppy, but Caldwell handled the boat with the confidence of a man who had made this trip many times. In her imagination, he might have been a ship's captain from centuries ago as he stood at the helm, feet braced in a wide stance while the sea breeze blew back his slightly overgrown hair. His gaze was fixed on the dark water ahead of them, and she had no intention of distracting him by sharing such wild thoughts. So, other than the hum of the boat's motor and the quiet rush of the water against the hull, they traveled in silence.

The ocean at night was disconcerting, especially when the moon was a mere crescent peeking out from behind heavy clouds only now and then. Even though she knew they weren't far from Key West, it seemed the black waters of the ocean were endless. It was amazing to her to think of how sailors in centuries past had managed to navigate such vast spaces where everything looked the same without the help of technology like GPS.

Just as Caldwell had promised, it wasn't long before Jayde could see the lights of Key West flickering at them across the water. She was about to take a deep breath in relief when the air lodged in her throat instead.

A thud against the fiberglass hull of the boat made her freeze in uncertainty. "Was that—?"

"Someone's shooting at us. Get down!" Caldwell's eyes went a little wild.

He grasped his police radio and requested backup. When dispatch had promised to send help, she brought his attention back to being shot at.

"From where?" Jayde asked as she tried to squeeze

herself down as low as possible in the boat. She still felt a little disoriented out in the vast dark waters.

He paused a moment before answering. "I don't know for sure. I haven't seen or heard any other boats. But we're too far from the island to be in range from there just yet."

"Someone was just sitting out here waiting for us? Anchored out to shoot us down when we came by?" Jayde's voice was muffled by the sounds of the boat breaking through waves that grew larger and larger as they approached the island's shoreline, but even that couldn't mask the high-pitched fear in her voice.

Another bullet splintering the shell of the boat was her answer.

"It looks that way." Caldwell pushed down the throttle and the watercraft lurched forward through the rising waves.

Jayde's head connected with the underside of the hard bench, momentarily stunning her. When she heard another boat motor starting up in the distance, she lifted her head for a moment to see if she could get her bearings.

Another shot convinced her to duck back down. The sound of the other boat growing closer was unmistakable. She stayed low beneath the boat's hull until she heard Caldwell shout above the roaring of the boat motors.

"Brace yourself," Caldwell yelled. "We're going to crash."

Jayde lifted her head just in time to see the other boat dead ahead and too close to avoid.

SIX

Caldwell jerked up the throttle and gave the boat's wheel a fierce tug to the right, but he knew they couldn't completely avoid the collision. A horrible wrenching sound filled his ears as the fiberglass and chrome on the bow of his boat raked down the side of the other craft. His boat teetered precariously, spinning a bit out of control. He reacted quickly, though, and punched the throttle forward once more. The other boat, a black speedboat with no lights on, spun around atop the water and jumped the waves while Caldwell recovered.

Jayde had a white-knuckled grip on the bottom edge of the metal bench she had been sitting on earlier. Her face was pale, and her eyes were wide, but she remained silent, strands of her auburn hair whipping into her face in the wind from the boat's motion.

He knew without even having to look that the other boat was pursuing them. He wasn't sure he could outrun the other vessel, but he would have to try.

Jayde waved an arm at him then, interrupting his thoughts. "I think we're taking on water!"

She was pointing at the floor of the boat up near the bow.

Her shouted words sent dread sinking through him. "How fast?"

But she didn't have to answer. A quick glance at where she pointed assured him it was coming in way too quickly. The collision must have damaged the hull. If they didn't make it to shore before it got too deep the boat could capsize and sink.

He tried to think quickly, but the pursuing boat and deepening waves were a ticking clock of distraction. He turned on the bilge pump and the backup pump to force as much water back out as possible. He couldn't risk stopping to attempt a temporary patch for the hole. They would be overtaken in seconds. It would be a race to shore. All he could do was try to keep the boat steady on course and moving as fast as he could safely manage.

The speedboat on their tail eased closer at a steady pace.

Caldwell had a new concern.

The other boat was trying to ram into them again, from behind this time.

Caldwell swerved, hoping he could make the other driver miss enough to prevent any further damage to his boat. When he swerved, however, the waterlogged boat tipped precariously to one side. It caught Jayde off guard. He tried to shout out a warning, but she scrambled to grab for anything to steady herself. Unfortunately, she was closer to the port side, which was tilted toward the water. Caldwell had no time to react as the boat lurched harder. A wave hit them broadside.

All he could do was suck in a deep breath before they were both pitched overboard. He heard Jayde's scream just before being submerged.

The cool water rushed over him. His life vest almost immediately bounced him back up to the surface like a bobber. He scanned the waves for Jayde, finding her wet head just above the waves a few yards away. He began to swim toward her. She seemed to be okay, so he searched out his boat as he continued swimming.

The boat had righted itself as soon as it had been relieved of the weight of its passengers, but momentum had pushed it several yards away from them. They were going to have to swim for it. Not an easy feat in the rough ocean waves.

The other boat had sped past as they had capsized, but the sound of its motor slowing then revving up once more didn't escape his notice. The man was turning around to come back toward them, a spotlight swinging back and forth across the water to locate them. Their bright orange life jackets with reflective tape had to be the reason he could find them so easily out here in the dark. The boat driver accelerated, clearly planning to finish them off.

Jayde noticed, as well. "What do we do?"

Her words were high-pitched, eyes wide. He had to figure something out and fast.

They wouldn't be able to dive deep enough to avoid the boat's motor with the life jackets on. They could shed them, but that might be too risky considering they would still have to swim at least to the boat. And the boat might not even make it to shore. He could swim away from her and force the other boater to go toward one of them or the other, but he couldn't risk Jayde being the one he went for. They needed protection.

And there was nothing out here but waves.

He scanned the open area, trying to think of a way they might use the waves to their advantage. He considered trying to force the man into turning directly into the waves in hopes of slowing him down. It would take a lot of effort to swim fast enough, but they could try.

When he looked back at Jayde, her eyes were closed, and her lips were moving. She was praying.

Caldwell looked back toward the boat. They might still have to dive. He was moving too fast.

"Shed your life jacket." He had to shout for her to hear him.

She opened her eyes. "What! Why?"

"Just do it. Hurry. We're going to have to dive. When he gets close, we'll dive down as deep as we can to avoid the boat and the motor. It's our only option." Caldwell had his life jacket almost off.

When she still hadn't followed his directive, he reached for the clasps of her vest.

"I've got it." She finally snapped out of it and brushed his hands away.

"Hurry!" Caldwell looked toward the accelerating boat.

Only a couple dozen yards stood between them and the rapidly approaching boat when he grabbed her hand and dove deep down into the water, dragging her along. He moved down and away from the boat's path. His grip on her hand was tight as he kicked to keep them deep below the surface until the boat had passed. Caldwell's lungs had begun to demand oxygen by the time they surfaced once more, in time to see the boat that had just missed them clip the stern of the sheriff's boat where the ladder groaned and snapped. Had he hit the boat again simply out of frustration? Or was he specifically trying to break off the ladder? They would have a tough time getting back inside the boat without it.

Caldwell looked around to get his bearings in the open water. Their life vests had been carried away by the roiling waves.

"To the boat. Swim as hard as you can." Caldwell didn't waste time looking around for the enemy boat. He let go of Jayde's hand she could swim ahead of him.

Thankfully, the waves carried them closer to their

boat. Jayde's prayers must have worked. The sound of a third boat approaching filled him with hope. Surely the guy wouldn't try to run over them with a witness. But they still needed to make it back to the boat.

Jayde's pace was beginning to slow, and her breathing became labored.

"Stay with me." He had to keep her going. "You're doing great."

She gave a little more effort, but they were still a good distance from the boat. He wasn't sure how they were going to make it. She stopped swimming.

"Just go. You can come get me when you get the boat. My arms are giving out." She was still close enough that he could see her weak attempt at a smile when he turned toward her, even in the darkness. "I can just float."

"I'm not leaving you. Besides, it's too dark and I might never find you again out here. Hang on to my back." He pulled her arms around his neck. Her grip was weak. Adrenaline must have sapped the last bit of strength she had after an already exhausting day.

"I can't." A wave almost knocked her words away as it hit their backs. He gripped her wrists to hang on to her.

"Yes, you can, Jayde. You have too much spunk to be taken down so easily. Just wrap your hands around me and hold on. I'll do the rest."

His words ignited enough motivation within her to prompt a response, at least. She clasped her shaking arms around him and allowed him to pull her through the waves, trying valiantly to help propel them with her kicking feet.

His muscles burned with the effort, but he kept pushing ahead through the briny water. The enemy boat was closing in again when Jayde's grip failed.

"No, no, no! We're almost there. Hold on." He tried to

catch her arms as her fingers slid apart. He missed and she bobbed into the water, sputtering as she resurfaced.

Hopeless fear clawed at him. Even if he could get her back to the boat, how would he get her back into it? It would be almost impossible if she didn't have the strength to help pull herself on board.

Focus on one problem at a time, he reminded himself.

He managed to get a solid grip on her again, and she wrapped her arms back around him clumsily. Where had the other boat gone?

Caldwell didn't have much opportunity to search while he pulled them both through the dark water. Once they reached his boat, he gently pried her hands away.

"Let me climb in, and I'll pull you on with me." He made sure she wasn't struggling to stay above the water before leaving her.

He could see in her expression that she was just as concerned about pulling that off as he was. He wasn't sure how they would balance their weight well enough to pull her up and into the boat without turning the boat over, especially with the water rapidly filling the bottom and both of them exhausted from the swim.

But they would have to try.

Getting into the boat was harder than he had anticipated with the waves rocking the vessel relentlessly. Without the ladder that normally extended into the water, he had to find anything he could to brace against to propel himself upward. Fortunately, enough of it had been left behind to allow him a decent handhold. He grasped it and pulled himself up, relying on his upper body to lift and balance the weight.

Once he had leveraged himself into the boat, he reached for Jayde. As he had feared, her grip was weak, and her body was tired. Whatever upper body strength had been left was lost while she had clung to him for the long swim back to his boat.

"Come on, Jayde. We don't have much time." He glanced toward the lights of the other boat.

She did, as well, and the sight clearly prompted a surge of adrenaline to renew her energy for a moment. She grasped hold of the boat and lurched upward, giving Caldwell enough momentum to pull her into the boat. The last few inches proved to be the hardest, but the struggle paid off.

She collapsed onto the flooded floor of the boat. It was filling more rapidly now that their weight was in the boat once again.

"Can we make it to shore?" She fixed her eyes on his face as she tiredly accepted the new life jacket he had pulled from storage.

"We're going to be fine. I'm going to call again for help." After snapping her new life vest in place, Caldwell picked up his radio as he put the watercraft into motion. A dispatcher promised a deputy was en route.

Sweat and salt water poured down his face. The other boat was still in pursuit. He had lost track of the third boat. He could only assume it had passed at a distance going in another direction. It was hard to tell in the dark.

Jayde was pale, even in the darkness. Her shoulder was no doubt burning and fatigue dragged her shoulders down.

"Just hang on. We should be there soon." Caldwell wished he could do more to bring her comfort.

His boat was starting to list to one side and drag. He kept the throttle down as much as he safely could, trying to make it to shore and outrun the black speedboat.

"Caldwell," Jayde whispered through chattering teeth. "I think we're going down."

* * *

Jayde swallowed back her panic.

She didn't know what would happen to them if the boat went down, and she didn't know how she would find the strength to swim for her life again in these brutal waves. At least she had a life jacket once more, but their attacker wasn't just going to let them float around out here indefinitely waiting for rescue. How were they ever going to reach the island?

She watched Caldwell's inscrutable expression as he surveyed the water coming into the boat. He looked calm on the outside. Was it a facade? Was he panicking on the inside, just as she was?

"Jayde, come back here behind the steerage with me. Make sure your life jacket is tight. We'll ride it out as long as we can, but I'm afraid we aren't going to get to shore before she sinks." He looked out over the water, now sparkling with the lights from the island ahead. As exhausted as she was, it felt like false hope to look at those lights—they were close, but not close enough.

The other boat tailed them for moments more before jetting away from the approaching shoreline suddenly.

"Why did he stop following us?" Jayde's teeth chattered as she spoke. Her wet clothing and hair seemed to catch every bit of wind as they coasted toward the beach, chilling her to the very center of her body.

"Probably getting too close to shore for his comfort." Caldwell shouted over the wind and boat motor.

Jayde only nodded, watching behind them in case the black speedboat returned.

The water inside the boat continued to rise, and her ankles were nearly submerged. Caldwell had to raise the throttle to keep them somewhat steady. "Come on. We're getting so close."

He seemed to be speaking to his boat, so Jayde remained silent. But she prayed under her breath just the same.

It made her wonder about his faith. She knew he had been struggling with some family things when he and Natalie met. But Natalie had never given details, just said she was afraid it would affect his relationship with the Lord. What that relationship was or had been, exactly, Jayde wasn't sure. She made a mental note to ask him if she got a chance.

She had struggled with her own faith after Natalie died. Her parents had considered it a part of the grieving process when she began to blame God, but His patience and persistence eventually won out. Jayde knew the Lord wouldn't let them go through such hurt without the promise of hope. And without the Lord, she hadn't had hope.

As she finished her prayer, looking up with thoughts of His faithfulness, her hope was restored. Another boat was surging toward them, this time from the direction of Key West. Flashing lights on the boat reassured her it was a county sheriff's vessel.

"Thank You, Lord," she breathed.

Caldwell flicked the lights atop his own watercraft to let the other boat know it was him. He raised the throttle the rest of the way until they came to a slow coast atop the water, waves rocking them sideways as they stilled. The other boat wound down, as well, as it got closer.

A uniformed man Jayde didn't know called over from the new boat. "Sir, toss me your line."

Caldwell did so quickly, then he began to help Jayde maneuver from their water-filled boat over to the new arrival. He followed right behind, a hand on her arm ready to steady her if she lost her balance on the rocking vessel.

He released her and she followed his eyes over to the

other watercraft. The intake of water had slowed without the added weight, but it was knee-deep now. It looked like it would be a total loss.

"Do you want to try to tow it in?" The deputy wore a confident expression. He wasn't new to traveling the ocean either apparently.

"Best to send someone for it." He explained the havoc that had just occurred quickly as the deputy prepared to head back to shore.

"Wow. I got a call that you were in distress, but I had no idea." The deputy eased down the throttle and the boat accelerated.

Jayde could only listen and shiver as she sent up a prayer of thanks for their rescue.

Jayde sat staring into a room full of uniformed deputies with a huge blanket wound around her, cradling her wounded shoulder. The salty ocean water hadn't helped the wound at all and the pain medication she had last taken over four hours ago was wearing off. The cold from the air conditioning still shuddered through her, though, and her still-damp curls were cold against her neck.

Officer Mendoza had been found in an abandoned stolen vehicle a mile from where he and his partner had attempted to apprehend the robber. He had been gagged and zip-tied after they had knocked him unconscious, but he would be fine.

Her waterlogged phone sat on a table next to her. She would have to replace the device as soon as she could, but for now they would have to rely on Caldwell's county-issued radio.

Deputy Ben Adams had let them off at the dock with Deputy Luke Mendoza and gone back out to help try to salvage the boat. Mendoza had driven them to the station.

Caldwell sat beside her in his own wet clothing, seemingly unaffected. He noticed her shivering and asked one of the men to turn up the thermostat a bit and bring her another blanket.

She sent him a grateful smile.

He had addressed the men in his department firmly, but kindly, explaining the need for help with catching Jayde's attacker. Most of the men wore concerned and interested expressions, but some didn't change their deadpan faces at all. One or two of them didn't attempt to hide their boredom. She didn't see Deputy Siebert in the group. She mentally made a note to ask Caldwell why he wasn't there.

"Deputy Gable, is there something else on your mind?" Caldwell spoke sharply, startling the unenthused man to attention.

"I'm sorry, sir?" The man who had looked so disinterested a second ago had the grace to look embarrassed.

"Your mind appears to be elsewhere." Caldwell wore a stern expression Jayde had never seen before.

A mumble came from the back. "Maybe his mind is on his ending shift."

Some of the men laughed. Jayde was filled with horror. Caldwell wouldn't like that remark at all.

But he surprised her by relaxing his expression. "I won't keep you from that new baby any longer, Deputy Gable. Be alert, men."

When most of the deputies had filed out, Jayde looked up to find a slender middle-aged man still waiting for Caldwell's attention.

Caldwell noticed him about the same time Jayde did. "Did you need something, Henry?"

"Actually, I wanted to ask about something." Deputy Henry's brow furrowed.

"What is it?" Caldwell glanced at Jayde.

"I hope I'm not overstepping, sir, but I think we're all thinking this might somehow be related to your late wife's death."

"I believe it is. Are you saying you no longer think Natalie's death was an accident?" Caldwell stood up a little straighter.

"I never believed it was, sir, just like you didn't. But I had nothing on which to base that theory…just as you didn't." He looked away for a split second. "I've heard talk. I don't know a whole lot about the history of Deadman's Cay myself, but there is a man who does. His name is Burke Pierce, and he recently moved to Key West because his health is failing. But he might be able to fill in some blanks." Deputy Henry gave Jayde a sympathetic nod.

"Thank you. Sounds like we need to chat with him. Know where we can find him?"

"I'll send you his address. He's in an assisted-living facility. And I'd appreciate it if you didn't mention this to anyone." Deputy Henry hooked a finger in the collar of his uniform and tugged at it just a bit.

"It will stay between us." Caldwell looked him in the eye.

He nodded his thanks before turning back to Jayde. "Nice to meet you, ma'am."

She returned the sentiment and thanked him, as well. Caldwell turned toward her as soon as Frank Henry walked out.

"That seemed odd. What is it about Deadman's Cay? It seems to be shrouded in mystery."

Jayde nodded her agreement. "More so than even I thought, and the island has always been a part of my life. I just hope this man will talk to us."

"We'll find out tomorrow. Right now it's already so

late. Let's find some dry clothes and a place to stay for the night and we'll regroup in the morning." Caldwell waved to the remaining deputies and a night dispatcher before leading her outside.

"I just hope we're trusting the right people." Caldwell spoke under his breath.

Jayde's blood chilled as she considered his words.

SEVEN

Caldwell made sure Jayde was up and ready bright and early the next morning, knocking on the door of her hotel room and telling her they would be leaving in ten minutes. She had grumbled something through the door at him about barely having time to brush her teeth, but he was anxious to see what Burke Pierce had to say. Deputy Henry had sent the address and the name of the assisted-living facility as promised.

"Towering Palms." Caldwell answered her question about their destination as they made their way down the sidewalk to a borrowed patrol car. "The assisted-living facility where we can find Burke Pierce."

"Perfect. Do you have something to record what he tells us?" Jayde scrambled to keep up with his long strides.

He held up a pen and notepad he had acquired from the front desk of their hotel. "Good old-fashioned pen and paper."

She chuckled. "Can I help?"

He started to reach for the door to open it for her, but he paused to nod. "Good idea. I might miss something."

"Do you mind sharing your paper?" She gestured toward his notebook as she crossed the threshold.

"Of course. I can play nice with others." He grinned and her chuckle nearly hung in her throat.

They rode in companionable silence as they cruised down palm-lined streets toward the assisted-living center. Caldwell turned on the radio, but commercials were on. He switched it back off.

Towering Palms was not only void of any towering palms, but you couldn't even catch a glimpse of water from ground level. It seemed a sad way to retire to an island to Caldwell's way of thinking. They entered the sliding glass doors where they were met with a cool blast of air. The early sun glinted off every available smooth surface, and inside, light flooded in through windows, painting the floor in myriad variations of the colors in the laminate. It seemed cheerful and well-maintained, at least.

"Good morning." A thin woman with a slightly hooked nose below her square glasses greeted them—with very little enthusiasm—from the front desk.

"Good morning, ma'am. I'd like to visit Mr. Burke Pierce. Would it be a good time?" Caldwell tried to be as polite as the receptionist had been indifferent.

But at the name Burke Pierce, her head shot back up from the screen she had turned her attention to after greeting them. "He sure does get a lot of random visitors. Are you with the writer guy?"

Caldwell turned to Jayde and lifted a curious brow. "I'm sorry. Did you say writer? Like, author of books? Or articles?"

"I guess that answers that." She looked back at the screen in front of her before continuing. "I don't know what he writes. I didn't ask. He just came in with a notebook and pencil, and you did the same. What's so fascinating about Mr. Pierce? He seems like a regular guy to me."

Caldwell pondered for a moment. He had worn plain clothes today. He could lie about their interest in the man. But it seemed pointless. Someone was bound to recognize him.

Pulling out his badge, he leaned toward her to speak in low tones. "I'm Sheriff Caldwell Thorpe. I need to speak with him."

She looked up again, and her eyes expanded behind the square glasses. "Is he involved in some kind of trouble? I knew all those visitors had to mean something."

"No, nothing like that." Caldwell was quick to reassure her. "But just how many unusual visitors has Mr. Pierce had lately?"

She seemed to think for a moment, and Caldwell feared she would refuse to say any more. But she finally spoke again. "Well. Not as many lately, I guess. Not since that young woman and her husband stopped coming to see him. Mr. and Mrs. Jones, they said. Cousins from the mainland or something."

Caldwell gave Jayde a suspicious look. "Did they have first names?"

"Yeah, but something common. I don't remember." She waved his question away. "Maybe you could ask Mr. Pierce."

"Yes, I'll do that. And the other visitors? You said there haven't been as many?"

She shrugged. "Just some younger man. He was alone. The writer guy. Mr. Pierce is in Room 115."

"Thank you." Caldwell turned back to Jayde. The woman had already gone back to her screen.

They followed the signs showing the room numbers and soon found themselves waiting outside a large oak panel after Caldwell knocked. The door was especially large—to accommodate a wheelchair if necessary, no doubt—and Caldwell was surprised to find such a diminutive man inside the room when he opened the door. Beyond the small fellow, a nice-sized room stretched out into a living area until it met a sliding glass door on the far wall. He couldn't see much more before the man grunted at them.

"More nosy reporters?" he asked. "Get the story from the other guy. I just wanna go to breakfast."

He flicked his hand out in a dismissive gesture.

Caldwell thought about showing him his badge but thought better of it. He didn't want to frighten the poor man. "I'm Caldwell Thorpe and this is Jayde Cambrey. We just wanted to talk with you for a few moments. Can we take you to breakfast?"

He squinted at them. "You wanna eat the breakfast they serve here? Ha! Glad somebody does. Not me. But I don't have a choice."

Caldwell fought to hold back a smile. "I'd be glad to take you somewhere else if it's allowed. Or we could go get doughnuts or something and come back."

"Doughnuts? I do love a good doughnut. Krispy Kreme, nice and hot. See you when you get back." He started to close the door and Jayde coughed. Caldwell was sure to cover a laugh. This guy was something.

"Just original, sir?" Jayde asked the question sweetly, and he turned to peer at her as if finally seeing her.

"What did you say your name was again? You look familiar." Mr. Pierce scrutinized Jayde until she cleared her throat.

"Um. Jayde. Jayde Cambrey, sir. My parents used to bring me to Deadman's Cay to vacation with my family when I was young." She smiled. "Did you know the Cambreys?"

He stood there a moment, deep in thought. "I think so. The house beside the Farleys, that big beach cottage with the bright blue roof."

"Exactly." Jayde beamed at him. "I was one of the little redheads running around causing trouble."

"Come on in. Your young man here can go get the doughnuts while we chat." Mr. Pierce reached for her and pulled her inside while Caldwell stood there stunned silent.

"Sir?" Caldwell said, but Mr. Pierce made a grunting noise and closed the door. Jayde hadn't corrected the man in thinking they were a couple. Caldwell turned away from the door thinking, *neither did I.*

The laughter bubbled out then. Caldwell made his way back down the corridor and stopped at the front desk. "I'll be back with doughnuts for Mr. Pierce. Would you like something?"

The woman behind the reception desk perked up immediately. "Oh, I sure love those chocolate ones with the sprinkles. You don't mind?"

Caldwell silently decided to bring back a couple dozen for the staff. "Not at all."

By the time he returned with a stack of Krispy Kreme boxes, he found Jayde and Mr. Pierce laughing in the common area. They had moved out to the bistro tables surrounding the coffee bar and sat chatting like old friends.

Caldwell could only shake his head. "Doughnuts."

Jayde smiled at him. "That's pretty obvious."

Mr. Pierce guffawed. "She's a sharp one. Did you know she was the valedictorian of her class?"

Caldwell smiled at her. "No, I didn't. I guess she only tells her secrets to you."

Jayde's face flushed and she looked away. "It wasn't a terribly large school. Mr. Pierce has shared much more fascinating facts."

"Is that so?" Caldwell tried to be nonchalant, as if he wasn't wanting to know everything the man knew about Deadman's Cay.

"For instance, he knew my grandfather way back in the days when they were boys, chasing adventure and telling wild tales." Jayde's eyes twinkled, and he knew she was more excited about something he had shared than she was letting on.

"Interesting." Caldwell tried to keep his voice neutral, but he looked around to see if anyone was within earshot. No one was. "And what about this reporter that you mentioned earlier?"

Mr. Pierce reached for the box of doughnuts that Caldwell offered up. Taking one out, he sank into it with a sigh of pleasure. He closed his eyes. "It's been way too long since I've tasted these amazing doughnuts."

"That box is all yours. Maybe you can sweet-talk one of the ladies into heating them for you later if you can't eat them all today." Caldwell grinned.

Mr. Pierce chuckled again. "I'd sure enough wind up in the hospital if I did. Too much sugar for one day. But thanks."

Caldwell thought he would have to ask about the reporter a third time, but Mr. Pierce swallowed and looked over at him.

"I don't think he was really a reporter." He took another bite.

His admission wasn't exactly a surprise, but Caldwell

was a little shocked Mr. Pierce would so readily admit that he knew this. "Is that so?"

Caldwell sat down while Mr. Pierce finished off another doughnut.

"I suspect he was after that pink diamond."

The background noise in the room seemed to fade away, and Caldwell swallowed hard, wondering if he had heard the man correctly. "The pink diamond? You mean the Rose Stone?"

Mr. Pierce nodded. "The two kids pretending to be a couple, too."

Caldwell tried to play it off. "I thought that was just a myth. Some kind of legend meant to drum up tourist visits or something."

Mr. Pierce cackled again. "I thought you lived there, boy? Look around. Do you think an island in the Keys needs much help attracting visitors? Beautiful islands."

He had a point.

"So you're saying there was really a pink diamond hidden on the island by pirates over a hundred years ago?" Caldwell studied him carefully.

"I might be old, boy, but I know what I saw." He took up another doughnut and began to dig in.

"You *saw* it?" Caldwell was beginning to think the man did have a memory problem.

He finished the doughnut. "Yep. Your wife did, too. Pictures, anyway."

Now Caldwell was really flabbergasted. "You knew my *wife*?"

Mr. Pierce looked at him guiltily, as if he hadn't meant to let that information slip out. "She used to visit me a lot on the other island, before I ended up here. I only saw her a few times after moving here. But she told me all about you. Showed me pictures. I knew who you were as soon as I opened the door."

Caldwell's head was spinning. "Why?"

"Why didn't I let on? Because I wanted Krispy Kreme doughnuts." Mr. Pierce chuckled.

Jayde laughed. "He's a sharp one...and was top of his class, too!"

Jayde watched the two men interacting and thought that it was good for them both. She didn't know who Caldwell had in his life in the way of mentors, but if he wanted one, she thought Burke Pierce would make one of the best he could ask for.

While Caldwell had been gone, she had learned so much about Mr. Pierce that she began to wish she could adopt him as her own grandfather. A little voice whispered, *you could, you know.* But she would have to go back home eventually. When she solved Natalie's murder.

Natalie.

The two men were talking about her now.

Jayde had no desire to try to compete with a ghost, even if that ghost had been her cousin. There could only be one explanation for Caldwell being so obsessed with solving Natalie's murder, right?

He was still in love with her.

True, she wasn't here to compete with her, but Jayde didn't want to be the *other woman* in any sense. If Caldwell still loved her...

It didn't matter. Jayde knew she wasn't in any place to love again. She didn't want any man in her life right now. Maybe eventually, but she wasn't ready. Not yet.

Mr. Pierce had already told her about the Rose Stone actually existing. She still wasn't sure she believed it. But if men were willing to kill to get their hands on it first, wouldn't they at least have some confidence that it was real?

She pressed a hand to her stomach. It was sickening what some people would do for money. Greed was one of the worst things she had ever encountered.

Natalie, no doubt, had thought it just a grand adventure, finding some legendary missing stone that most people scoffed at. Jayde could just imagine Natalie's excitement. She had always loved the history of the island.

Caldwell's voice broke into her thoughts. "Jayde?"

"What?" She looked up, knowing her expression must show her confusion. "I was deep in thought."

"I see that. I asked about the stories your grandfather told you about the Rose Stone?" Caldwell tilted his head slightly. "But maybe I should ask what thoughts had you so engrossed."

She ignored his last reference. "He did tell us stories, but the legend was the story we asked to hear most often."

"What legend is that?" Mr. Pierce was looking at her curiously.

"The legend that pirates had hidden the Rose Stone somewhere on the island of Deadman's Cay. That they had stolen it from British naval sailors who were transporting it for their princess. The pirates had been seen and were running for their lives when they literally sailed into Deadman's Cay. Their ship sank, but they managed to make it to shore with the Rose Stone. The naval officers caught up to them, though, and while they had already hidden the stone, none escaped with their lives." Jayde shook her head sadly. "All that for a shiny rock."

Mr. Pierce chuckled again. "Yes, it was a waste, but that part of the legend isn't what I was referring to. The pirates deserved what they got. But not everyone who touched the Rose Stone may have gotten their comeuppance."

"What do you mean?" Jayde couldn't hold back her enthusiasm for hearing more of the story. She watched Mr. Pierce's expression carefully. "I thought that was all there was to the legend."

Caldwell's face had shuttered. Was he afraid of what Mr. Pierce was going to say? Afraid it involved Natalie somehow? A shiver trembled through her.

"No, but that was no doubt what incited two islanders to go looking for the stone in later years. That, and rumors that it was worth millions, maybe even billions of dollars. But the story says that there were two men working together—one with the money and the other with the brains. But one of them was betrayed by the other, and both died without ever cashing in on their victory." Mr. Pierce let his voice fade off, and Jayde realized that was all there was to the story.

"No one knows who the two men were? Or what became of the diamond?" Jayde shook her head sadly as Mr. Pierce answered her.

"No, but there was talk that it had been hidden. That whoever betrayed their partner claimed to have lost it. But some say it's still hidden somewhere on the island. That's what Natalie was trying to find out." Mr. Pierce looked at Caldwell.

"And you told her what you've just told us?" Caldwell looked up from where he was jotting down some notes.

"I did. But she told me a couple of things, as well." His tone had turned secretive.

Jayde straightened in her chair. "About the Rose Stone?"

"In a way, yes." He turned toward Caldwell then. "The last time she came to visit me, she acted differently. A little frightened, even. She said there was a chance you might need to know some things later on."

Jayde watched Caldwell's face carefully. "She was afraid something might happen to her?"

Mr. Pierce's expression drooped. "I didn't know it then. But yes, looking back on it now, I think she might have suspected someone might try to harm her."

Tears pricked at Jayde's eyes. Why hadn't Natalie told them? What reason could she have had for keeping this to herself?

"What did she say I might need to know?" Caldwell asked.

Mr. Pierce glanced around the empty room as if suspecting a spy in their midst. "She said to tell you there is a hidden room in the attic."

"That's it?" Jayde didn't know how that would help them.

Mr. Pierce's face twisted into a grimace. "She also said to tell you *trust no one*."

EIGHT

After they left, Caldwell played around with the idea that Natalie had been talking about Jayde when she said not to trust anyone. It didn't take him long to dismiss the thought, however. He had only gotten to know her these past couple days but working in law had taught him to trust his instincts. And his instincts said that Jayde wasn't capable of that kind of dark betrayal.

They had taken a ferry boat back over to Deadman's Cay after talking with Burke Pierce, rather than risking it alone again. Once they reached the island, they went to get Jayde another phone before they headed for Rose Stone Cottage on foot. Caldwell was on high alert all the way, but the tension in his shoulders eased as they approached the front door. He was about to breathe a sigh of relief that they made it back without any problems when he noticed a window on the side of the house stood open.

He knew neither he nor Jayde would have been that careless, not after all that had happened.

He laid a restraining hand on Jayde's arm as she reached to unlock the door. "Wait. Something isn't right." He pointed to the open window. "Let me go in first."

She stepped back as he drew out his Glock and removed the safety. He eased the door open slowly, leading with the weapon. He kept Jayde in the corner of his eye while he visually scanned the room, tensing at the sight before him. When he eased in enough for her to see past him, Jayde gasped.

The cottage had been ransacked.

"Shh. Whoever did this might still be here," he whispered to Jayde. "Stay behind me."

He moved through each room of the house with Jayde at his back, finding every room in a state of disaster. Drawers were dumped on the floor, furniture had been scattered and overturned, cabinets and closet doors were left hanging open, and the perpetrator had even gone so far as to tear down most of the wall hangings and Natalie's paintings, throw the cushions on the floor and toss the rugs aside. Mementos and knickknacks lay in smithereens on the floors. Destruction was everywhere, as if a vengeful beast had torn through the house in uncontrolled rage.

Glancing behind him, he saw that Jayde's face wrenched and reddened as she fought back tears and anger. He didn't doubt her thoughts ran along the same lines as his. Why? Why would anyone do this?

How had that someone known they had left the island? *And what had they been looking for?*

After looking into every room, upstairs and down, Caldwell finally spoke.

"They're gone." His flat voice sounded angry and harsh to his own ears. Fury welled inside him, replacing the adrenaline that had surged at the possibility the intruder remained. He breathed in deeply, schooling his temper.

She stood beside him, fist clenched, her body shaking. "This isn't just a scare tactic. Whoever it was seemed to be looking for something. And when he didn't find it, he took out his anger on the cottage."

Tears streaked her face.

"I think you're right. Is Natalie's journal still hidden?" He walked to the guest bedroom and found the secret wall safe untouched.

"Maybe they couldn't find it?" Jayde's brow furrowed. "But why would they be so desperate to find her journal? Do you think they were looking for something else?"

"Like what? The stone? How could they know if she even found it or not?" Caldwell had to fight to keep his cool. The disaster that was his home was devastating. He wanted to go after the villain and make him pay. Not just for this, but for terrorizing Jayde. And, if his instincts were correct, for killing Natalie. He had crossed every line, violated nearly everything there was to violate.

Jayde sank down on the edge of a chair that had been stripped of its cushions but somehow left upright. Her cheeks were damp with tears, and she closed her eyes and shook her head. "I don't know, but they seemed desperate. Do you think it was more than one person?"

"It could have been. I'm not even sure whoever broke into the cottage and tried to attack us wasn't working for someone else. Just don't touch anything. I'll have the place dusted for prints. I doubt they left anything behind, but I want to make sure." He pulled out his radio but thought better of it. "Let's go to my friends Parker and Amelia's first. We can't stay here."

"Wait." She surprised him with her reluctance. He didn't want to look at the destruction any longer, and he didn't think she would want to, either.

"What for?"

"Remember what Mr. Pierce said? What if they come

back? What if they find the room he spoke of before we return?" Jayde rose from the chair.

"You're really that concerned? If we had to be told, how do you think anyone else would find it? It might not even be anything significant." Caldwell shook his head. He felt a headache beginning to throb behind his eyes.

"If it wasn't, why would she want to make sure you knew?" Jayde splayed her hands out as if laying out the clues.

Caldwell sighed. "Look, Jayde, I didn't want to tell you this at first, partly because you didn't trust me, but also because I was embarrassed. I think Natalie was going to ask me for a divorce before she died."

Her face changed completely. "What? I thought you said you two were happy."

"The truth is, we were struggling. At first, I thought she was just homesick for her parents. Then I said some harsh things… I accused her of being a moody artist. But I finally realized I was being judgmental, and I began asking her what was really wrong. If she knew how to fix things, she wouldn't tell me. I did everything I could to try to make her happy. But one day she told me she just wasn't happy, and she needed to figure out how to address that. I assumed that meant she was going to see an attorney. I was miserable waiting for her to just do it, and I grew resentful of her in turn. I never dreamed she'd be killed before we could figure something out. This room… It could be something to do with her desire to be separated from me." Caldwell didn't want to look at her, to see the disappointment and accusation there. He had seen a similar expression too many times in Natalie's eyes.

He saw Jayde's face soften out of the corner of his eye. He had mentioned similar concerns to her before. But he hadn't told her the full extent of his and Natalie's marital problems. Did it shock her?

If so, she didn't react. She leaned closer and took his hand. "I'm sorry, Caldwell. I know that must have hurt you deeply."

The warmth and softness in Jayde's touch sent a tenderness swirling through him that he wanted to latch on to and never relinquish. It was comfort and contentment all wrapped up in one moment, her gesture splitting his hardened heart down the middle.

He couldn't help looking up at her then. Her eyes reflected his own emotions back at him, with a deep empathy he had never experienced from any other woman. But how could he put her through what Natalie had endured? It might have been his fault that Natalie wasn't happy. What if he wasn't a good enough man, a good enough husband? What if he couldn't make Jayde happy, either? What if things started off great and then deteriorated into misery like his relationship with Natalie had?

It was too much to risk. He wouldn't take the chance.

He swallowed hard and reached down deep. Once he had control of his outward display of emotions again, he laughed, though it sounded cruel to his own ears. "I'll be fine. Let's go check out this secret room before we leave, then. Might as well know now rather than later."

Jayde didn't understand what had happened.

Caldwell had opened up to her. That fact lodged itself in her hopeful heart and wouldn't let go. But then something had changed. She had watched him, seeing the raw emotion, the tenderness filling his eyes.

And then he had closed it all off once again.

What had she done? Was she too much of a reminder

of Natalie? Even if she wasn't, would he always compare her to her cousin, anyway?

It wasn't fair to have to compete with a dead woman. There was no winner in that game. She might as well let whatever infatuation she was developing for Caldwell go right now. Even if their marriage was already going poorly before her death, Caldwell had still been in love with her cousin at one time. Regardless, Jayde didn't want to disrespect Natalie's memory by getting involved with Caldwell...no matter how much she was growing to like him.

She attempted to redirect her thoughts as she followed him up the stairway, the only part of the cottage that hadn't been ransacked. When they reached the studio upstairs, she saw that it was in as horrible shape as the rest of the house, with Natalie's paintings and sketches tossed haphazardly about the room, easels overturned and paint tubes oozing out their pigments all over the rugs covering the floor.

The far wall of the studio was smeared with red paint, as if the intruder had grown angry enough to leave a chilling calling card that mimicked blood. Macabre handprints in the smears of paint surrounded aggressively drawn letters that read, Where Is the Stone?

Caldwell looked around for just a moment before stepping over the mess on the way to the studio's bathroom. He didn't outwardly react to the violent mess that was formerly Natalie's special place in the cottage, but he also didn't linger in the carnage. When they reached the bathroom door, he motioned for Jayde to show him the way into the attic.

"She said there is a secret room *in* the attic, correct? Or is the secret room just the attic?" Caldwell was watching as she stepped into the closet of the bathroom and carefully lifted out the simple board shelf. In the back of the closet, there was a support board that stuck out from the wall. Jayde ran her hand along the under side of it and searched for the trip latch to the attic door just below.

"*In* the attic, I think. That's what Mr. Pierce said. Now, if I can just remember how to get this door open, maybe we will be able to figure out where the hidden room is." Jayde reached around inside the closet, under the shelves and around on the wall. She had been just a girl the last time she had snuck up here to hide with her cousin.

"I'm not sure we should do this right now. If it's difficult to find, we might have to come back later." Caldwell was frowning at the shelf she had just removed. She had the feeling he didn't especially want to deal with this right now.

She didn't intend to give him a choice. She was far too anxious to put this whole mystery behind them.

"Aha!" Jayde tripped the latch and the door leading away from the back of the bathroom closet swung inward. It was more of a crawl space at the opening, and Caldwell eyed it warily.

"It widens once you get in there," Jayde reassured him.

"Alright. You first, then." He still sounded skeptical.

"Sure. It's not as creepy as some attics I've seen." Jayde led the way.

It was only a little dim in the brightness of day, but Jayde used her phone's flashlight, anyway. It made her feel like she could see a little better.

"Ow!" A dull thud alerted her to Caldwell's difficulties getting through just before his interjection did.

"Are you alright?" Jayde asked, a note of amusement creeping into her voice.

"I'm fine." He grumbled the words.

"It must be terrible to be so tall." Jayde's voice held a healthy amount of teasing.

"You have no idea." He lumbered along behind her, rubbing his head.

"Well, it's safe for your head in the rest of the room." She had stopped at the edge of the attic room and stood, hands on her hips, looking around. "You've never seen any of this?"

Caldwell shook his head as he came to stand beside her, his mouth hanging open just a bit. "What am I looking at, exactly?"

The attic had the typical boxes and storage tubs in one corner. But in the middle was a wide array of old furniture, steamer trunks, books, globes and all sorts of academia. A telescope lay on its side atop a chart mapping the stars, and even a ship in a bottle, such as he had only seen once in person. Everything was coated thickly with dust, giving Caldwell the impression someone had hoped it might all be forgotten.

"Some would call it my grandfather's collection. But when he passed, my grandmother wouldn't allow anyone to touch any of it." She shrugged. "I guess after that, none of us wanted to betray her wishes, even after she was gone."

He picked up the ship in the bottle. "This is modeled after *The Angelica*. It's the ship the pirates were rumored to have been on when they stole the Rose Stone."

He held it up, and sure enough, *The Angelica* was painted right there on the hull of the tiny ship. Jayde sucked in a breath.

"That's interesting." She stepped closer and looked at the intricate details. "It's so amazing that anyone can even create these. I find it fascinating."

"I've seen bits of them being created. It looks tedious to me." Caldwell chuckled. "But they are very cool."

"What's this?" Jayde picked up a leather-bound book beside the star chart. She flipped it open, and the old, tired pages began to crumble at the edges. She immediately pulled her hands away in case she might damage the brittle remains. "Is this a replica of the ship's log?"

Caldwell peered over her shoulder. "That's too old to be a replica. Look at the parchment it's made of. It's practically turning to dust." He set the ship in a bottle down to get a closer look. "Jayde," Caldwell whispered, "I think that's the actual logbook from the ship. Why isn't that in a museum somewhere?"

She set the fragile book back on the dusty table as gently as she could manage, awe filling her. She delicately flipped to another page, revealing the folded map Jayde had mentioned earlier. Natalie must have put it in there after writing about it in her journal.

But Jayde was more interested in the piece of history before her now. Shutting off her flashlight, Jayde began to google ship's logs from *The Angelica* on museum websites. A photo appeared at the top of one of the searches, and when she held it beside the book, they could only stare.

Caldwell turned on his flashlight. "How can it be?"

Jayde closed out the photo and scrolled through more results. An article a few lines down caught her eye immediately. "Look at this."

She pulled up the article.

"Ships' Logs and Other Artifacts Stolen from Museum," it read. Farther down it mentioned *The Angelica* and the legend about the pirates stealing the Rose Stone.

"How did your grandfather come to possess a stolen ship's log from an ancient vessel rumored to have possession of the very stone that was supposed to have been hidden on this island?" Caldwell's eyes narrowed as he skimmed the article and looked back at the book.

There was no doubt it was one and the same.

"I don't know. But I think we need to find out."

NINE

Caldwell gaped at their findings.

They hadn't even found the hidden room yet. What other surprises was Natalie hiding?

His anger at her flared before he could remind himself that he shouldn't bear ill will toward the dead. He took his dad's advice and squashed the fury. He wouldn't dwell on what either of them should have done. It was fruitless.

But he did intend to find out who had known what Natalie was up to. Whoever it was seemed to be enthralled enough by the idea of getting their hands on the Rose Stone that they were willing to kill.

"We should just return this to the museum." Jayde was shaking her head and backing away as if she didn't want any part of whatever her grandfather had been doing.

He was thinking along the same lines. Whatever Farley had been up to, he couldn't have gotten these artifacts through honest means.

"I agree. The museum needs to get this back. But we need to figure out who was so desperate to get their hands on it they would kill Natalie." Caldwell looked around the room as if the answer might materialize.

"Wouldn't it still be okay to go ahead and return this, though?" Jayde's brow furrowed.

"It might be better to use it as bait first." Caldwell carefully opened the ship's log.

"Wouldn't someone have already found the stone if it was mentioned in the log?" Jayde moved some maps and charts around on the old desk.

"Maybe. Unless they didn't really know what they were looking at." Caldwell kept perusing the pages as if something might jump out at him.

"Or unless they found it and then hid it again, like the rumor Mr. Burke mentioned." Jayde looked around the room. "But I don't know how there could be a hidden room in this attic. It's so small, anyway."

Caldwell blew some dust away as he peered at the other items on the desk. "That might be part of the reason it is so small. Look at this."

He gently lifted a spyglass from the table. Beside it lay a compass, both with a matching leather outer binding, the same as the logbook. Jayde stopped looking around and looked more closely at the spyglass in his hand. "It's engraved."

Tiny letters stamped into the leather near the bottom were near impossible to read due to the wear of time and the elements. Caldwell ran his thumb back and forth across the lettering, silently willing the leather to spill its secrets.

Jayde let out an awed sigh. "Wow. Do you think there's any way to find out who it belonged to?"

Caldwell squinted at it. "I'm sure a historian could determine the name without damaging the artifact. But remember what else Natalie told Mr. Burke."

Jayde was nodding. "Yeah, that's true. But for all you know, *trust no one* might have included me. What can we do?"

Caldwell replaced the spyglass on the table. "I have an

idea. But we will have to be very careful. I'm pretty confident we could find the information we are looking for on the internet, but if someone else is diligently searching for the stone, or even these artifacts, searching on any of our own devices is risky. The public library has internet access. You can pay cash to use it for a few hours. No one could trace it back to us if we used their servers."

Jayde pondered a moment. "Won't there be cameras? Could they ask the librarian who had used that computer?"

"I don't think they would take the risk of asking. It would expose them, as well, if they did. And the librarian is a stickler for maintaining privacy." Caldwell picked up the compass and turned it over.

"What if someone follows us? Could they look over your shoulder and see what you were looking up?" Jayde ran a hand over the ship's log again as if to remind herself that it was real. Her expression said she knew she was starting to sound a little paranoid, but she couldn't seem to help it. The attacks had her shaken.

"We'll have to take the chance. We've already googled *The Angelica*. We might as well just try to stay one step ahead of anyone who suspects us. It's already apparent someone thinks we know something." Caldwell gestured toward their phones.

"Okay, let's go as soon as we find this room, then. Can you help me check the walls for any unusual seams or other tell-tale signs of a hidden panel?"

Jayde was already feeling her way around the attic walls, peering closely at the surface as she went.

"Of course." He put their findings aside and strode over to the opposite side of the room. Whatever secrets the attic held, it didn't seem to want to give them up easily. He checked the shelves while she made sure there wasn't anything odd about the floor.

They searched fruitlessly for a half an hour before Caldwell decided they might need to take a different approach.

"I think maybe we should move on to the internet search. Maybe if we focus on something else, an idea will come to us." Caldwell ran a hand through his thick brown waves.

"You're probably right. I'll think on it." Jayde put a hand to her lips. "What are you looking for on the internet?"

"I'm going to see if I can find any videos or instructions on how to learn what's stamped here. And I'm going to look for some recent articles about the artifacts. I plan to contact the museum, as well." Caldwell turned for the door.

"Is that safe?"

"If the email is from an anonymous law enforcement agency." Caldwell grinned. "If they're looking to acquire the stone illegally, they wouldn't want to arouse the suspicion of the police."

"You can do that?"

"Of course. We have our ways. A privilege of being the sheriff. I know a few tricks. We have tech specialists to help us block identity without losing integrity."

"Will the museum answer your questions without knowing who you are? What if they don't trust you?"

"Then we'll go there in person."

Jayde hated to admit it, but her desire to continue this adventure was waning. The idea of traveling to the Deep South Maritime Museum held little appeal to her. In fact, she was afraid of doing so. They had been followed everywhere else and attacked. If they were caught out on that kind of excursion, their attacker would become much more desperate. The closer they got to figuring this out, the more danger they were in. She hoped they wouldn't have to go to the museum.

Caldwell was right, though. They couldn't waste time. It drove her a little up the wall that they still hadn't found the secret room. What if they were missing out on a clue by not finding it first? But when she had asked Caldwell, he had assured her it would still be there if they needed it.

Also, she was distraught over the mess in the cottage. She didn't relish the idea of trying to clean it up and put things to rights with her aching shoulder. "Are you going to just leave it? What'll we do about sleeping arrangements tonight? Will we be staying at a hotel again?"

He grinned at her. "You're a planner, aren't you?"

She stopped her racing mind for just a moment and just looked at him. "What?"

"You know. Someone who likes to have the whole agenda laid out ahead of time. Not comfortable with spontaneity?" Caldwell motioned for her to follow as he started back through the attic entryway.

"Is there something wrong with that?" She felt he didn't mean it as a compliment.

"Nope. Just an observation." He ducked through the entrance.

"Are you a—a planner, as you put it?" Jayde still wasn't convinced.

"No. I like to have a plan, but I'm totally okay with it changing. In fact, I kind of expect it." He waited for her outside the little door, extending his hand for her.

"It doesn't bother you when plans change?" Jayde didn't understand how he could be so okay with it.

"I figure it's part of life. Things are never going to go

exactly as we plan. Too many external factors. So why get all upset about it if things will inevitably change?" He shrugged as she waved off his hand. He closed the door behind her and made sure it was secure.

They made their way out of the bathroom and back into the studio. When they started down the stairs, she finally spoke again. She couldn't let it go so easily. "Yeah, but it's still upsetting. Sometimes it's more than upsetting."

He stopped and looked at her. "It is. But I just don't dwell on it."

She shook her head. "I wish I could do that. Just shrug things off like that."

He simply shook his head, and they continued down the stairs. "A difference in personalities, I suppose."

She pondered that thought as they made their way back down the stairs. The waiting mess filled her with myriad unpleasant feelings as she looked around the cottage. So much damage… How could someone do this?

"I'm going to take you to Parker and Amelia's for now. If we need to stay overnight, I'm sure they won't mind. We'll go to the local library tomorrow." Caldwell kept a slow pace down the stairs, taking in the damage again, as well.

"So should I get my things? If they aren't scattered everywhere, that is." She winced.

"Probably best if we both do. I don't think you need to stay here tonight no matter what. And if we end up going to the museum, we'll have what we need." He went to get a few things of his own as she ducked into the guest room.

Her room looked almost as bad as the living room except they hadn't done as much vicious damage here. There were no slashes or rips in her belongings, though the bedding had all been stripped off and the mattress sat partially off the bed at an odd angle, as if the intruder had looked under it and just left it where it fell. The drawers from the dresser and nightstand had been turned upside down and tossed aside. The closet, too, had been thoroughly searched. All her personal belongings had been discarded in scattered piles all over the room. The scent of the perfume she had recently purchased permeated the room with a stifling intensity.

Jayde felt tears welling up in her eyes as the sense of violation filled her anew. To think of some stranger so carelessly going through her things made her stomach churn with nausea.

But standing here crying wouldn't help. She bent and began collecting the bedding. Setting the mattress fully atop the bed once more, she straightened it and piled the comforter, sheets and pillows in the middle before she began to pick up her clothing. Under a small pile of her personal belongings, she found the shards of the glass perfume bottle the intruder had cruelly shattered when he knocked everything from the top of the dresser.

She was holding the pieces in her hands, looking at them in horror when Caldwell appeared in the doorway. "You doing okay?"

"Such needless destruction." She shook her head as her face turned toward his. "It was only perfume, but it's the unnecessary violence. Why be so cruel?"

Caldwell crouched beside her and took the sharp pieces of glass carefully from her hands. "A person who would do something like this has a darkness somewhere inside that can't be easily remedied. It swells with anger and hatred, and eventually it spills out into the world around them. They want others to hurt along with them, as if it's some kind of penance for the rest of the world to have to share their suffering. They don't really know who to blame for their perceived misfortune, so they want to make as many people as possible pay for their personal pain."

"But something *could* fix it. If they would only give the Lord a chance, don't you think His love could quiet the anger?" Jayde stretched out her now empty hands, palms up.

"Yes. I believe His love could. If they would let Him in. But sadly, many don't understand the free gift that's been bestowed upon them. They believe they're too far gone for repentance and forgiveness. And often, people just don't know how to change." Caldwell stood and reached for her hand.

"It's so sad. The world could be a better place, if only…" She accepted his hand.

He nodded. "Can I help you find what you need?"

She gave him a sad smile. "Thank you, but no. I'll only be a few minutes."

True to her word, Jayde had her packed bag ready to go less than five minutes later. Caldwell took it from her arm, and they closed the door on the ugly havoc in the cottage for the time being. Her face was drawn, but she walked briskly beside him as if nothing was wrong. She could only hope he was fooled by her actions.

She didn't want to confide in him about it, but something about the museum made her feel anxious, as if by involving the curators they were exposing themselves to more danger.

But she wasn't sure how.

Caldwell had looked up from his phone when she had emerged from the bedroom, disclosing that the email had been sent. For no explicable reason, it had sent a chill down her spine to think they had just exposed themselves in such a way. If someone was truly so desperate to get their hands on the billion-dollar stone, they could be watching the correspondence coming in and out of the museum. For all she knew, it could be the museum curator himself.

Jayde was tired of sounding paranoid, though, so she vowed to keep her concerns to herself. After all, with his background in law enforcement and criminal law, surely Caldwell had already considered everything she could think of and more.

Once they reached the home of his friends, Parker and Amelia, she relaxed just a little. Amelia was warm and friendly, even though she kept sending knowing glances toward Caldwell. The Hensleys were the epitome of Southern hospitality, though, offering her food, drinks and anything else she could need.

Caldwell told them about the intruder at the cottage, and Amelia and Parker volunteered to help with cleanup. It was one of the wonderful things about the small island. Neighbors took an interest in the welfare of others. Jayde had no doubt that many others would show up to help, as well, once they learned about the incident.

Once the men had disappeared to the back patio, however, Amelia smiled at her with a gleam in her eye. "Caldwell sure is acting differently lately."

Jayde sucked in a deep breath and stepped back a half step. "What do you mean?"

Amelia smiled at her, though. "I mean he's actually smiling. He let you stay in his cottage. He brought you here to keep you safe."

"I don't understand." Jayde felt her brows draw together on her forehead.

"I think he likes you." Amelia continued smiling, but

the door opened, and whatever else she might have said was forgotten.

"I'm going to grill us some burgers. Do you want to make something to go with them?" It was Parker directing the question at Amelia, but Caldwell stood just behind him, his eyes searching Jayde's face. It was almost like he was looking for clues to her welfare.

She shot a smile in his direction to show she was fine. Did he know what Amelia had been discussing with her? She hoped not. Heat flooded her cheeks, and she looked away.

"Of course! We'll whip up some sides and something for dessert." Amelia sent a loving smile toward her husband.

Jayde felt a small tightening in her chest as she watched the exchange. It was obvious the pair was deeply in love, and Jayde couldn't help wondering what it might be like. She knew her parents had been in love once, but now they seemed to live separate lives. Was that what happened to every couple after years of marriage? She wanted to believe otherwise, but she wasn't so sure.

"How long have you been married?" Jayde asked Amelia. She had offered to help in the kitchen, and Amelia had set her to chopping vegetables for salads.

"Five years. But we were high school sweethearts. Before high school, really. We've had our ups and downs, but I have no doubt he loves me as much as I love him." Amelia looked up from the recipe she was reading for chocolate truffle cake to answer. Her eyes lit with happiness as she talked about her husband.

"Wow. That's a long time, and you seem so happy together." Jayde hoped the note of envy wasn't as apparent to Amelia as it was to her.

But Amelia just smiled a secretive smile as she went about making the cake.

"Oh, we are. We have our squabbles, just like everyone else, but it all comes out in the wash. The main thing is we're both willing to look past the other's faults, forgive and say we're sorry." Amelia went to the pantry for an armful of ingredients.

"My parents have been married a very long time, but they seem to simply tolerate each other these days." Jayde hadn't meant to say such a thing out loud, but it was out before she could take it back.

Amelia looked up from her recipe once more. "Oh, I know what you mean. But I'm sure they still love each other deeply. Does it concern you?"

Jayde hesitated. "I guess I'm just not sure that love really lasts. Not anymore, anyway. The whole world just sometimes seems so...so selfish."

"In some ways it is. But not everyone. And I believe that love can last, as long as a couple works together to keep their relationship a priority. Honestly, I love Parker more and more with each day, week and year that passes. I never thought I could love him any more than I did when we first became a couple." Amelia turned to the window where she could see her husband outside at the grill chatting with Caldwell. "And despite how things might have soured with Natalie, I do believe Caldwell is capable of that kind of love. He's a good man."

Jayde wanted to say she agreed, but it stuck in her throat.

"Were you and Natalie friends, as well, then?" Jayde wondered if she was prying too much. After all, they had only just met.

"I suppose we were. She wasn't really close to anyone here, though, so I wouldn't say we were confidants.

But the growing tension between Natalie and Caldwell was obvious. And he confided in Parker and me, mostly asking for our advice." Amelia looked back at Jayde with a gentle smile.

A small part of her was envious that Amelia had known Caldwell so much longer than she had. She and Parker obviously knew him well, if he had confided in them about how his relationship with Natalie was floundering. Of course, he had been married to her cousin before, so it wouldn't have been possible for Jayde to be close to Caldwell before now, anyway. The errant thought brought back to her mind how out of line she felt emotionally right now. If she were thinking more clearly, surely she wouldn't even consider thinking of her late cousin's husband so personally.

A tiny whisper reminded her that it wasn't anything inappropriate to feel a fondness for Caldwell. He was a widower. She certainly hadn't had an emotional connection to him when Natalie was still alive. In fact, she had honestly rather disliked Caldwell on their first and only meeting prior to Natalie's death. She smiled to herself at the thought.

A clearing throat reminded her that Amelia was still watching her, and that she had failed to respond. "I'm sure he is a good man. I don't plan to stick around for long once we get this thing all sorted out."

"So you *are* working together trying to solve the mystery around Natalie's death." Amelia dropped her knife and beamed at Jayde. She wiped her hands on a dish towel and got down a couple of glasses. "I thought so."

Jayde noticed she hadn't exactly said the word *murder*, but Amelia was definitely suggesting some foul play had been involved. Or at least that something mysterious had happened to her. Jayde didn't press the matter, though. Sometimes it was best to start by listening to what wasn't said.

So Jayde skirted the subject as she watched Amelia make two glasses of rich, amber-colored sweet tea. "We just decided it might be best to pool our resources."

"Well, I hope you won't listen to the locals. I know many of them still think Caldwell was somehow involved. They still whisper about it. But they don't really know Caldwell. If they did, they would know what a good man he is. He would never have hurt Natalie." Amelia took a sip of her tea.

Jayde didn't mistrust Amelia, but she felt uneasy discussing the topic with her at present. "Honestly, I haven't really met anyone but you and Parker. And Ty, the deputy, and he seems quite loyal to Caldwell. We've spent too much time avoiding whoever is trying to keep us from figuring this whole thing out."

Parker came in the back door then. "Could we get a platter? The burgers are almost done." He waved his spatula around crazily.

Amelia laughed. "Sure. You don't know where they are?"

He made an ornery face at her, but there was a definite note of teasing in their banter. "Fine, I'll get it. You were just closer."

"And you wanted to get back to your buddy." Amelia dodged in front of him to get the plate out of the cabinet. He grabbed her around the waist as she went by and landed a quick kiss on her cheek. She laughed before getting the plate.

He grinned as she handed it over and gave her a sweet kiss on the cheek. "Thank you, darlin'."

He exaggerated his drawl, and both ladies laughed as he ducked back out the door.

The conversation turned to more mundane matters as Jayde helped Amelia finish preparing the sides, but Jayde's mind kept circling back around to what Amelia had said. Why did the locals mistrust Caldwell? Was it just because he was an outsider?

She finally put the question from her mind. Amelia was right. She had seen no evidence at all that Caldwell was anything but a good man.

"How's your shoulder healing?" Amelia asked as she prepared the icing to add to the cake later.

"It still hurts often, especially when my pain medicine wears off. But I can at least use it a little more easily. The stiffness from the swelling is improved." Jayde didn't ask how she had known about what happened. She assumed Caldwell had told Parker.

Amelia had the cake in the oven just in time, and they gathered up the macaroni salad and vegetables they had whipped up and took them to the outside table near the grill.

They ate on the patio and still sat beside their empty plates, exclaiming over how delicious everything was, when a foreboding darkened the air around them with a near tangible presence. Everyone grew quiet, and Jayde looked over at Caldwell. He had gone completely motionless, head tilted just slightly as he listened.

When his trance-like demeanor broke, it sent a ripple of fear through Jayde.

"Everyone in the house. Now."

TEN

Everyone scattered at once, and the crack of gunfire sounded just yards away.

Caldwell watched the women disappear into the house out of the corner of his eye as he dropped below a low garden wall coming off the raised back patio, pulling his gun as he rolled in close. He thought the shots had come from the beach side once again. Whoever was after them apparently found it easier to stalk them from the water. He needed to find out what boats had been out frequently the past couple of days. It was likely there was more than one man involved and someone was dropping a partner near the shore to approach from the ocean side. Would someone really take the chance of anchoring out in a close vicinity frequently like that, knowing Caldwell was going to be scouting the island's perimeter? Or were they making the drop and abandoning their partner to whatever fate they suffered?

The answer that came to mind chilled him. They wouldn't care about anchoring out or otherwise if they thought Caldwell would be dead before he could look into it.

He was beginning to suspect whoever was behind these attacks had an in at the county sheriff's department. It was nothing but a hunch right now, but he had learned long ago to trust his gut. The attackers knew his and Jayde's every move. It was more than a coincidence.

He resolved to exercise greater caution. He had to stay alive to protect Jayde. He couldn't let another woman down. Natalie's death had been a hard lesson, but he would make sure it wasn't in vain.

Parker had disappeared into the house, as well, but Caldwell knew it had only been to retrieve his own weapon. Before Caldwell could make another move, Parker came creeping up from the front of the house, low and silent. He made it to cover just before another shot was fired, and he shot Caldwell a cheeky grin and a thumbs-up as he settled into his place behind a large wooden planter housing several ferns.

What's the plan? He mouthed the words.

Caldwell looked toward the beach, then gestured. He watched Parker's face and knew the instant understanding dawned. He shook his head fervently.

Caldwell nodded. He knew it was risky, but he was going to have to try.

He eased out from behind his cover, testing the shooter's attention. No shots came, so he sent Parker a signal to cover him.

"You've lost your senses!" Parker sent the remark hurtling toward him at a stage whisper. He rewarded him with a grin of his own.

He ducked low and made a break for new cover closer to where the shots were coming from. He made it to a small storage shed farther down the beach just as another shot echoed across the sand.

Parker's return fire produced a yelp.

Caldwell wanted to shout out a compliment about his friend's skills, but he kept quiet. He would have to remember to tell Parker how great the shot was later. He eased out farther while the man was tending to his wound, but Parker's words made him stop in his tracks.

"Bro. Someone's trying to get in the house."

He didn't bother to whisper this time, and Caldwell mentally kicked himself. Of course. This shooter was just a distraction. The real danger came from the man going after Jayde.

He didn't bother to stay low this time but sprinted back to the house with every bit of strength and speed he had. Shots ricocheted around him, but he had a singular mission.

He had to protect Jayde at all costs.

Parker spoke as he rushed toward the new attacker, but he didn't register any of his words. He flew into the figure and knocked him to the ground.

Stunned, the other figure could only twist and turn, trying to free himself from Caldwell's angry grip. He let out a cry when Caldwell twisted his arm, shoving it behind his back. "Who are you?"

The angry growl did nothing to persuade the man to do more than grunt in protest, and Caldwell twisted harder. "What do you want? Why are you here?"

He knew the answers, but he wanted to make this guy say it. He wanted him to suffer.

A shot pierced a window of the Hensleys' home just then, though, and a scream from inside brought his mind back around to what he needed to do. Another shot and a cry of pain from Parker had him on the offensive. He knocked the weapon from his opponent's hand before slamming a debilitating fist into the intruder's face and shoving the limp man face down at the ground before running to help.

"Parker!" He called out to his friend who had been trying to crawl up the back steps to get to the women.

"I'm hit." Parker stated the obvious. Blood pooled on the jeans across his thigh, and Caldwell sucked in a horrified breath.

"I've got you man. Hold on. It's gonna be alright. I'm calling for backup now."

"My wife." Parker's expression was anguished.

"Amelia's fine. I'm sure of it. We'll get in the house, and you can see for yourself. Can you walk?" Caldwell wasn't sure how they would make it into the house at the slow pace his injury would require without one of them being hit again, but he had to try.

"Hurts. Not good." Parker's face had lost all color. From the angle of the broken flesh wound, Caldwell was afraid the bullet was lodged in his friend's thigh. He had to get him somewhere fast to control the bleeding. They were in a mess to be sure.

"I know, brother." Caldwell grabbed a small piece of driftwood beside the patio, probably intended for an evening fire. "Here. Bite down on this. We have to get you in the house."

The unconscious man hadn't stirred, but an occasional shot still came from the beach.

"Leave me. Take care of the ladies." Parker was shaking his head, not accepting the stick.

"Not a chance. Now, bite down." Caldwell stuck the stick close to Parker's mouth once more as he gave the firm order.

Too weak to argue further, Parker did as he was told. He tried for a couple of steps, but Caldwell ended up bearing most of his weight across the patio and up the steps. A shot ricocheted near Caldwell's head as he beat on the door.

Amelia opened the door and screamed in fright, eyes wide at the sight of her husband's wound. She rushed toward him.

"He's alive, but we have to get him inside." Caldwell shoved the door open wide. "Stay back. He's still shooting."

Another shot proved his words as he tugged Parker into the back door. Jayde came running to help him. He wanted to chastise her for not doing as he said, but he was too grateful for her help.

Amelia slammed the door closed as soon as Caldwell had Parker inside. He fell against her, mumbling. She laid her head against her barely conscious husband's chest, speaking loving words of reassurance. Tears streamed down her cheeks. Another shot shattered a window beside the door, and she couldn't hold back another shriek.

"Amelia. I need something to use as a tourniquet and bandages until we can get him to the hospital. Can you find me something?" Caldwell thought she needed a distraction as much as he needed supplies.

At first she didn't respond. Jayde grasped her arm. "Amelia? Do you want to tell me where to find them?"

She shook her head. "I'm going."

Jayde had her phone to her ear as soon as Amelia was off. "I'm going to make sure they are sending an ambulance." She gave him a look of horror then. "There's no hospital on Deadman's Cay."

"They can take him by helicopter." Caldwell carefully watched his friend fading in and out of consciousness. He looked at the wound as closely as he could without hurting Parker more. "I think the bullet is still lodged in his thigh. He'll need surgery."

Jayde spoke to the dispatcher as Amelia came running back in with the supplies she had. The gunshots slowed, as the shooter must have realized his accomplice wasn't holding up his end.

"What now?" Jayde asked, an edge of desperation in her voice.

Caldwell was still working on Parker's wound. "Take my phone from my pocket and call to check on our backup."

"What? How—how do I do that?" Jayde stared at him as he worked at stopping the blood flow.

"I should've had you ask the dispatcher. Just call Ty. His number is there. Even if he isn't on duty, he'll come." Caldwell tried to keep his cool, but his best friend had been shot and he had two ladies depending on him to keep them safe with two men still out there trying to harm them. He couldn't quite temper his tone.

"Okay. I should've thought of that. I'm sorry." Jayde was searching for Ty's number.

"'Melia?" Parker barely got his wife's name out.

"I'm here. Hang on. We're going to get you to the hospital." Amelia stroked his hand as tears rolled down her face.

"Fire in my leg…" Parker groaned.

"They're on their way. Just rest and keep on being tough." Caldwell spoke this time as Amelia's face contorted.

"He's going to—"

Another shot broke off his words. They all jumped at the sound of cracking glass in the patio door. Jayde yelped in the middle of explaining the situation to Ty.

Caldwell could hear Ty yell that he was on his way through the phone just before Jayde disconnected.

"He's going to be okay, Amelia. I'll make sure of it." Caldwell finished what he had started to say earlier. She nodded in response, a grateful yet tearful expression on her lovely face. She looked terrified, and Jayde looked pale and frightened, as well.

A seeming eternity passed with nothing but an occasional gunshot. Amelia prayed over her husband, and Jayde squeezed her hand. Caldwell kept constant pressure on the wound until his hands began to cramp from the effort.

He heard the chopper first, but sirens sounded just after them. Ty was pounding on the front door in seconds, lights illuminating the fractured windows in a vibrant show of red and blue.

Jayde let him in as soon as she verified it was him, and Ty rushed to where they had been caring for Parker near the back door. They hadn't moved him far for fear of making the bleeding worse.

"The guy you cuffed is headed to the station. The other shooter's gone. I sent another deputy to police the area. Chopper's landing in the empty lot across the way. Medics will bring a gurney as soon as the bird hits the ground." Ty spoke so rapidly it took a moment to process what he had said.

Pride in Ty swelled up in Caldwell. The guy was young, and some of the other men had thought him too timid to do the job. But in a moment of need, he had stepped up and taken charge.

But Caldwell didn't have time to dwell on that right now. He had to get his best friend to the hospital.

He commanded a couple of deputies to stand guard as the medics brought the gurney in. He insisted they give Parker something for the pain right away, and once they had him loaded onto the gurney, he ran alongside right up to the belly of the chopper, even though Parker was mostly unconscious.

"Watch your head!" A medic yelled the warning as they drew closer to the rotating blades.

Caldwell ducked, squeezed his friend's hand, and then helped Amelia into the chopper beside her husband, making sure she kept her head nice and low. She would ride with him to the hospital and send them updates as soon as she received them from the doctors.

He stepped way back and stood beside Jayde as the chopper took to the sky. He grasped her hand before looking over at her. She had tears rolling down her face.

"This is my fault. If I hadn't come here and started digging into Natalie's death, this wouldn't have happened." She stood rigidly holding his hand and staring after the shrinking lights of the helicopter.

"How do you know it wouldn't have happened anyway? I was looking into it myself. It just so happened we both started digging around the same time." He spoke low and gentle to her, close to her ear.

She shivered and turned toward him. Fear for her continued safety and relief that she was okay right now mixed in a confusing knot within his chest. But he couldn't deny the tender feelings he was feeling for her right now. Her closeness only intensified them, and when her green eyes fixed upon him in the flare of the lights, he had no power against the need to pull her closer.

She didn't resist, and he was struck by the feel of her sweet frame nestled against him and how perfectly she seemed to fit into his arms. They simply embraced, clinging to each other for comfort as the surge of adrenaline ebbed at last. It felt like home in a way he had never experienced, and it shook Caldwell to the core. How was he going to deal with this? He would long for this feeling for the rest of his life after this.

He didn't let go, though. He would savor it as long

as he could. He let it wash over him and solidify in his memory. He would cherish the memory of having sweet, soft Jayde Cambrey in his embrace forever. He closed his eyes and sighed.

A throat cleared, bringing him back to reality. "All clear, sir. Would you like a ride somewhere?"

Ty's innocent question reminded him of the destruction waiting back at the cottage. Now Amelia and Parker's home had suffered damage, as well. He could sleep in his office. He had done so before. But what would he do for shelter for Jayde?

"Um, let me make a few calls." He explained to Ty what had happened back at the cottage.

The deputy sucked in a breath. "Wow. I'm really sorry to hear that. We have some room at my place if you need somewhere to stay for a night or two. Looks like the Hensleys' place will need some repairs, as well."

Caldwell considered for a moment. "Thank you, Ty. But I think maybe it might be best if I get Jayde off Deadman's Cay for the night. If we need a place to go tomorrow evening, we might just do that."

Ty nodded. "The offer stands. Just let me know if you need a ride."

He turned to walk back over to his patrol car, but Caldwell halted him. "Deputy."

Ty paused to look back at him.

"Good job tonight. You handled the situation like a pro." Caldwell gave him a nod, smiling slightly.

Ty flushed. "Thank you, sir."

He nodded at Jayde before walking away.

"So we aren't staying on the island tonight?" Jayde looked up at him.

"You aren't. I have deputies on the other Keys and the mainland. I'll find someone else to protect you tonight."

He didn't look at her directly, but he could feel her response like it was his own.

She was angry.

Jayde could do nothing but stutter for a moment. How could he plan to abandon her right now?

"You—you gotta be kidding me! You c-can't leave me right now." She hated the fear and desperation she heard in her voice, but she had been through too much tonight to consider leaving Caldwell's side.

"I'm not abandoning you. I'm going to go to the hospital in Key West and sit with Amelia and Parker." He spared her a brief glance that revealed nothing.

"What if I want to go, too?" Jayde's stance widened, and she crossed her arms.

"I thought you didn't want to put them in any more danger." It seemed to be the only argument he could come up with.

"And I suppose you don't think you're any danger to anyone? You just said you were as much to blame as I am." Jayde pulled herself up taller. "Unless you were just saying that to make me feel better."

Caldwell blew out a long breath. "I guess you've got me there. I'm just thinking of you. I didn't think you'd be thrilled with the idea of sleeping upright in a hospital waiting room."

"Well, I'm sure you aren't, either. But I'd like to know how Parker is, too." Jayde's arms slid back down to her side. "Like it or not, we're kind of in this together. Might as well make the best of it."

Something in his expression changed, and she felt like she was seeing a part of Caldwell that hadn't surfaced in a long time. "You're right. I'd probably only worry about you all night if someone else was looking out for you tonight, anyway."

"You want something done right, you gotta do it yourself, right?" She gave a little chuckle. "Isn't that how the saying goes?"

His vulnerable expression morphed into a smile. "If you have a strong need to be in control, I guess so."

She slapped his arm lightly, his teasing finding its mark. "I might."

He laughed then. "I might, too. Who's going to win the power struggle?"

She leaned into his arm, but then wished she hadn't when his warmth made contact. "Maybe we can take turns."

Long after she leaned away again, the feel of Caldwell's arm against her own stayed with her. It was warm and tingly, and she didn't know how to stop herself from wishing for a good man like him in her life. She had decided a few years back that she probably wouldn't marry. She liked doing her own thing, not having to answer to anyone and only being responsible for herself. She wouldn't deny that sometimes that life had been a lonely one, but she did have a few friends to go to dinner with from time to time. Her parents stayed busy traveling and entertaining their friends, but she still saw them occasionally and on holidays. If her life felt empty at times, it was probably her own fault.

When her cousin had died, she had been forced to re-evaluate that plan, wondering if her life would have any real meaning if she lived it on her own. She wasn't sure how to change that plan without it affecting every aspect of her life, however, so she hadn't given in to the urge to do so. Friends tried to set her up on dates occasionally, but she had most of them convinced that she was fine on her own. If they shook their heads at her in consternation, well, they didn't make a lot of fuss about it.

Ty had taken them to another county-owned watercraft, and they were now headed to Key West once more. The trip was uneventful this time, for which Jayde was grateful. She knew their attacker was probably just using the evening to regroup before trying again, but she was glad to be able to catch her breath, even if worry for Parker and Amelia clouded her thoughts.

When they reached the dock at Key West, a deputy waited for them with a patrol car. Taking them to the hospital, he promised to bring another vehicle for Caldwell and leave it in visitor parking.

Taking the elevator to the third floor, they navigated a long corridor before finding Amelia pacing in a waiting room.

"He's in surgery. The doctor promised to let me know as soon as they're finished." Amelia was pale, but still seemed much better than she had been when they had left her with the helicopter crew.

Before either could respond, Jayde's cell phone rang. "I don't know this number. I'd better answer, just in case."

She stepped back out of the waiting area as she spoke her greeting into the device.

A sharp reply came from the other end. "Jayde, this is Tristan. I hear you've been trying to reach me."

She was silent for a moment, unsure of what to say. She hadn't left any kind of message for her cousin, and she hadn't expected to hear from him. "Um, hello, Tristan. I hope I'm not intruding on your time. How did you know that I'd called?"

"My assistant said a woman had called claiming to be my cousin. You're the only female cousin I have. It had to be you unless the caller was lying." His brusque tone did nothing to set her at ease. "I only have a moment."

His offhand reference to Natalie's death made her gut clench in anger. He had never been an especially loving person, but this just seemed callous, even for Tristan.

"Of course. I won't waste your time. I was simply wondering if Natalie had by chance contacted you before her death. There are some strange things going on around the island." Jayde spoke carefully.

He grunted. "I don't know anything about it. She might have tried to call, but I never talked to her. If she called, she didn't leave a message, either."

A dig at Jayde. "I wasn't really offered the option to leave a message. But it doesn't matter. I'm just trying to find out what really happened to her. I know our family had some issues, but I thought she might have contacted you."

"I would say 'issues' doesn't begin to describe our family. Dysfunctional is certainly a word that works, though. Do you even know why your mother and our grandfather didn't get along?"

Jayde sucked in a breath. "What do you mean?"

"Never mind. That's a story for another time."

Jayde was tired of his arrogance. "Listen, I'm sorry I bothered you. Thank you for taking time out of your busy schedule to call me back."

He made a half-hearted sound of acceptance. "And Jayde? If I were you, I'd be careful on that island. Some said the rumors were just legend. But some said the island was cursed."

"I don't believe in that sort of thing." She laughed softly.

"Maybe not. But I'd still be careful if I were you."

He disconnected, leaving that cryptic warning between them.

Jayde stared at her phone screen for a moment before returning to the waiting room. She felt rattled by his words. Something about his manner had seemed intimidating.

"Is everything okay?" Caldwell studied her as she entered the room, stepping closer to her.

"I'm not sure. That was my cousin, Tristan. I think he might've just threatened me."

ELEVEN

Caldwell might have thought she was joking if her face hadn't been so pale. But the sincerity of her fear was undeniable. He thought her hand shook as she returned her phone to her back pocket.

"What did he say?" Caldwell eased her into a chair.

"Just that he hadn't talked to Natalie, and to be careful." Jayde dropped the phone in her lap, just staring at it.

"That doesn't sound all that threatening." Caldwell tried to lighten the mood, but it didn't help.

"It was the way he said it. He mentioned some thinking the island of Deadman's Cay is cursed. I told him I didn't believe in that sort of thing." Jayde looked up at him at last.

"Well, it is named Deadman's Cay. I suppose it's not that unusual for superstition to play a role in that. Or vice versa." Caldwell wasn't quite convinced.

"That's true. But why call me at all?" Jayde hugged her arms around herself, her linen blouse crinkling beneath her protective stance.

"Can I ask you something a little more personal?" Caldwell looked over at where Amelia stood, close enough to hear snippets of their conversation. She seemed absorbed in something on her phone.

Jayde seemed a little uneasy, but she nodded slowly. "I suppose so. What do you want to know?"

"Why didn't your grandfather leave the island and the cottage to everyone? I mean, why only Natalie's father? Was he the old-fashioned type that thought inheritances should go solely to the male of the family?" Caldwell winced to even say the words. It seemed harsh in this present day.

"Not exactly. I never got the full story, but Tristan's mother, Felicity, received business ownership as most of her inheritance. My mother got another property. But it was never any secret that Natalie's father was Thurman Farley's favorite child. My mother was something of an outsider in the family, really. She didn't get along at all with her sister, Tristan's mother. I know my grandfather and my mother argued often. I just don't know what they argued about." Jayde dropped her arms and turned away for a moment. "She seemed upset when he died, but I was young enough that I took it only as grief at the loss of a parent. I've often wondered if it was more than that. Did she regret the tension in their relationship still existing at the time of his death? I just don't know."

The comment hit Caldwell painfully in the chest. He didn't want that to be how things ended with his mother and his brothers. He had to figure this whole thing out, and soon. "Have you asked her?"

Jayde's expression turned to surprise at the question. "No, I guess I never really thought about it."

Amelia moved closer to them then, and Caldwell let the conversation go as he saw the look on his friend's face. "How're you holding up?"

Amelia scrunched up her face. "I'm okay. I just can't help wondering what's taking so long."

Caldwell gently touched her hand. "Take it as reassurance that the doctors are doing a good, thorough job. He's going to be fine."

She offered him a grateful smile, and Jayde, too, nodded her head when Amelia's worried gaze met her face.

"I'm so sorry this happened," Jayde said quietly.

"Please don't blame yourself. My husband has always liked to be a hero. So has this guy. It's bound to have some repercussions sometimes." Amelia rolled her eyes after indicating Caldwell.

Caldwell looked at Amelia, opening his mouth to make a smart retort, but before any further exchange, a doctor in scrubs entered and spoke Amelia's name.

"We're all done, Mrs. Hensley. Everything went well. It'll be a lengthy healing process, so take it easy on him for a while. A nurse will give you the care instructions for the next several weeks. Call me if there are any problems." She nodded at Amelia from beneath her scrub cap, blue eyes full of sincerity.

"Thank you, Dr. Manderly." Amelia shook hands with the female surgeon and turned back to Caldwell and Jayde.

"That's great news." Caldwell folded Amelia into a hug and felt her sag with the weight of relief. "Now you can get some rest."

"I'll try, but I do want to stay close." Amelia's smile was full of exhaustion. No doubt the worry was taking a toll on her.

"We'll be here, too. I promise one of us will wake you if Parker needs anything." Caldwell gave her shoulder a brotherly pat.

A half hour later, they had Parker settled into a recovery room where he would stay overnight in case of any complications. Caldwell tried once more to talk Jayde into going to a hotel to rest, but she wouldn't hear of leaving them.

So they settled into a couple of recliners in the hospital waiting room for the night.

Though the hospital was pretty quiet by a little after 10:00 p.m., Caldwell had trouble sleeping. He found he spent most of the night watching Jayde sleep in the recliner beside him, while Amelia slept in the one beside Parker's hospital bed in the private room.

His thoughts started out mundane enough, but before long he was trying with all his might to put together the clues they had collected about Natalie's death. If he had still had any doubts someone had murdered her, those doubts had all been laid to rest as soon as the attacker began shooting at Jayde. He wasn't sure why they hadn't attacked him before then, other than he had done his best to keep his investigations quiet.

And it was hard to miss the arrival of a lady as lovely as Jayde Cambrey on the island. It seemed unlikely she would just decide to come for a visit all of a sudden when, according to Natalie, Jayde hadn't been back to Deadman's Cay in years. She had apparently begun a successful college education and gone right into an equally successful career in advertising, living in Atlanta near her parents. Coming back to the island had never seemed to interest her before now.

Jayde didn't look like the cutthroat professional Natalie had described, especially now while she slept. But she *had* gone after the truth with a single-minded determination that was rare in many people of late. He admired that about her. She didn't really take no for an answer.

They needed to get back to the cottage and find that room Natalie had told Mr. Pierce about. From what he had told them, those artifacts were just the beginning.

Had Natalie somehow found the diamond? Was that what had actually put her in danger?

He didn't think so. But something in the attic was important to putting this all together. The journal was one piece that they needed to examine more closely. Why hadn't he thought to bring it with them? He could be reading it now for clues, instead of sitting here trying to conjure the truth from nothing.

It was around four in the morning when he finally dozed off. He was awakened three hours later by his buzzing cell phone.

"Ty? What's up?" He tried to hide his grogginess when he answered the phone, but it was still obvious he had been sleeping.

"I'm sorry to wake you, sir. A man was just caught poking around your cottage. He claims to be a relative, so we're calling for verification of that." Ty's tone indicated he didn't at all believe the man was a relative of Caldwell's.

"What? Who is it?" Caldwell sat up straight in the recliner.

"His identification says he's Tristan David Vaughn. He says he's your late wife's cousin."

Jayde heard Caldwell speaking to someone on the phone, but her mind was still hazy from sleep. She knew she must have been dreaming it, but she thought he spoke her cousin's name.

She sat up and looked at him.

He looked furious and began talking rapidly into the receiver.

"Hold him until I get there. I don't care if his prints and ID both match who he says he is, find some way to keep him until I can get there. I'm on my way." Caldwell was sliding his boots on even as he spoke.

"What's going on?" Jayde rubbed her eyes, trying to focus.

"Your cousin just got caught poking around my house. Grab your stuff. I need to have a chat with him." He didn't wait but picked up her handbag for her while she was still struggling to sit up and put on her shoes.

"But he just told me—"

"Lies, apparently. It looks like he's decided to try to find some evidence for himself. Maybe he sent the guy who wrecked the cottage. Maybe he's been behind this the whole time. But it's time to get some answers." His expression was mutinous.

Jayde tried to get her shoes on quickly while Caldwell stalked to the door of Parker's room and knocked. She assumed he was simply telling Amelia what was going on.

He was backing out of the room and asking her to keep him updated about the time Jayde finished with her shoes and stood.

Taking the patrol car the deputy had promised the day before, they drove, with lights and sirens on, to the dock as fast as they safely could. Jayde was barely getting fully awake when they hopped into a county sheriff's department boat and sped across to Deadman's Cay. She was thankful for no unexpected attacks this time, as she wasn't sure how she would have functioned in an emergency in the state she was in. Fatigue wracked her brain, and she struggled to achieve full physical function, as well. What was wrong with her?

Caldwell seemed to have no such issues. His obvious anger only seemed to have subsided a little by the time they reached Ty and Tristan. She watched his face as he looked over her cousin with a tight-lipped stare.

"What are you doing here, Vaughn?" His clipped tone reminded Jayde that he was accustomed to dealing with hardened criminals. She wrapped her arms around herself to ward off the chill that coursed through her.

"I don't have to talk to you. My lawyer's not present." Tristan's thin frame bore just as much stiffness as Caldwell's.

"You lied to me on the phone." Jayde spoke this time.

His gaze flickered over to Jayde, softening a bit. "I didn't exactly lie. I might've avoided the truth a bit."

"What truth is that?" Caldwell took an imposing step toward him.

"Again, I don't really feel the need to talk to you. You can speak to my lawyer. What, exactly, are you still holding me for, by the way?" Tristan smirked at Caldwell, pointedly staring at his name badge.

"You were trespassing." Caldwell snapped the words out.

But he wanted to wipe the smirk from Vaughn's face. Of course, he wouldn't be able to hold him long before he was out on bail, and Tristan knew enough about law that he wasn't going to let Caldwell get the upper hand so easily.

Jayde tried again. "Tristan, just tell us what you're doing here. What do you know?"

Her cousin sighed. "I don't know anything. I was at the cottage looking for you. I knocked on the door and there was no answer, so when I noticed the broken window, I went to investigate. I thought you might be hurt."

Jayde wasn't sure if she believed him or not. "Why were you here looking for me? Last night you gave no indication that you were anywhere near Deadman's Cay. We haven't spoken in months, maybe over a year before that. All of a sudden you are so concerned you're here looking for me?"

He had the grace to flush a bit. "I know we've all been busy. I should've told you last night I was coming. But after I spoke to you, I had a bad feeling. I felt like I really needed to get here and check on you. The broken window just confirmed my intuition. I knew there was something wrong."

She crossed her arms over her chest. "I'm fine. But I don't understand why you didn't just tell me the truth. You could've called back or texted me to tell me you were coming."

He looked at Caldwell, and for a split second she thought she saw a flash of anger pass over his features. But then he blew out a breath and shook his head. "I thought you were all alone here. I should've known you'd have Thorpe protecting you."

His tone bore just enough insinuation to make her suspicious. "What do you mean by that?"

Tristan shrugged. "Just that he's the sheriff. He would want to be the hero even if you weren't his wife's cousin. As it is, he seems to like overly curious redheads."

The remark stung Jayde, just, she thought, as he had intended it to. She turned away.

Caldwell had stiffened beside her, though, and his low words came out dangerously flat. "I'd hate to think you're insinuating anything derogatory toward Jayde. If you only mean to insult me, fire away, but I won't have you insulting her."

Jayde could scarcely absorb his chivalry, however, for her mind was homing in on the similarity of Tristan's words to those of the note left in the bottle beside Natalie's bicycle. *Nosy redheads end up face down in the ocean.*

It replayed in her mind to the point that she felt a bit

dizzy. Nausea swelled in her middle. She almost missed Tristan's reaction.

"Thorpe, you really need to learn how to behave like a gentleman, rather than some backwoods Neanderthal. Ladies like to defend themselves these days." Tristan's snarky tone did little to hide his opinion on the matter.

Caldwell's reaction came as slightly less than a snarl. "Get lost before I do something that might endanger my career. But rest assured, whether you stick around or leave, I'll be watching you."

Tristan blinked rapidly, trying to put some distance between himself and Caldwell, who had stepped closer to issue the warning. His demeanor spoke of a definite urgency to get away. "Is that a threat, Thorpe?"

Caldwell didn't bother to even look around at their audience. "Take it however you will. But if you're up to something, I *will* find out."

Tristan shrugged it off and turned to leave. "Oh, I wouldn't dream of upsetting the island. It has enough dark history without my adding to it, even if I wanted to. Maybe it's you that Deadman's Cay needs protection from."

He pierced Jayde with a long stare before turning to go. She stared back, but whatever it was lurking behind his overly confident smirk, she didn't like it at all.

She shuddered as he strode away.

TWELVE

"He's hiding something."

Caldwell didn't look at Ty or Jayde as he issued the statement, but he could feel their body language, and it was tense. They didn't have to nod to let him know they agreed with him.

Ty put a clenched fist close to his mouth, looking like he was deep in thought for a moment. "I don't know why, but it seems like I've seen that guy before."

Jayde shook her head. "Surely you couldn't have. Not here, anyway. Tristan hasn't been back to the island since he was fifteen. Not before now."

"You're sure of it?" Caldwell asked.

Jayde nodded. "Yes. He spent his birthday here, but he and his family got into a big fight. He was an only child. He said he was never coming back to the island again, and according to his mother, he never has."

Ty shrugged. "Maybe he just reminds me of someone else."

Caldwell didn't comment, but he tucked the information into the back of his mind. Maybe what Jayde had said was right. Or maybe that was simply what Tristan Vaughn wanted everyone to believe.

"Let's head back to the cottage. We should finish up

what we were doing before we return to Key West to check on Parker." Caldwell directed the words toward Jayde.

If she noticed he no longer felt he could trust her safety to anyone else, she didn't mention it. It wasn't that he didn't trust Ty, but he wanted to stay close to her himself. Caldwell couldn't put a finger on when it had happened, but somewhere along the way he had decided he needed to be the one to protect her, even though he still had niggling little doubts about whether he could do a good enough job. And he didn't want to weigh the meaning behind any of it.

"Of course." She seemed a bit distracted. Caldwell only hoped she couldn't read his thoughts. "Um, thank you, Ty."

After Ty's acknowledgment of her thanks, Caldwell led her down the sidewalk toward the cottage. He kept a vigilant watch for anything suspicious, but he noticed Jayde paid little attention. It was a warm fall day and the sun was shining. It looked anything but ominous, but Caldwell knew they had to be prepared no matter how seemingly peaceful their environment might be. It was often deceiving.

Jayde was eyeing a particularly tall palm tree along the beach, head tilted back as she studied it. He couldn't explain his sudden irritation, other than he couldn't comprehend why she wasn't taking the situation more seriously right now. She wasn't even watching their surroundings.

"I'm glad you feel so safe in my presence, but two pairs of watchful eyes might not be a bad idea." He made the quip under his breath, but she snapped to attention.

"Oh, right." She looked away from the palm tree, and her head began to swivel from side to side.

"May I ask what's got you so distracted?" He shortened his long strides to accommodate her smaller frame as he realized she was hurrying to keep up.

"Same reason you aren't really talking much, I'd assume. Just wondering what Tristan is really up to. He never gave a reason for wanting to see me after he gave that excuse. Nor did he give any reason for being here. It's so random. Or, well, I feel like it's not really a coincidence." Jayde's words were hushed, but they came out in a rush.

"No, not a coincidence at all. What all did he say when you talked to him last night? Tell me everything." Over the sound of the crashing waves, Caldwell could hear the squeals of laughter from children playing on the beach not far away. The island had always been such a happy place and a safe haven...until Natalie's death. He wanted it to go back to how it was before, though he wasn't sure it could ever be the same for either him or Jayde.

"He really didn't say anything, other than what I've already told you. That he hadn't talked to Natalie, and that I should be careful on this island—which now I'm thinking that the first part is a lie." Jayde let out a sound that was half huff, half sardonic laugh.

"I think he nearly had to have talked to her. And with what Ty said about him looking familiar... I think he looks guilty of something." Caldwell stopped to speak to an elderly lady who was sitting on her porch. The woman had simply waved, but he called out a greeting.

"Your purple hibiscus looks prettier every time I pass by here, Ms. Regina."

She giggled back at Caldwell. "Thank you, my dear."

Jayde smiled up at the woman while the two exchanged a few more words. Caldwell introduced them, and Jayde called a greeting to the woman, as well.

"Nice to meet you, Ms. Regina." It earned her a smile and similar sentiment.

They walked on, and Caldwell waited a few beats to speak once more. "Do you remember Mr. Pierce mentioning all his visitors?"

Jayde nodded. "Do you think Tristan was one of them?"

Her chest felt tight when she considered how they might have put the older gentleman in danger somehow. She sincerely hoped the security was good at the assisted-living center.

"I think it's a very good possibility. I'd like to go back and ask him."

"When we go to check on Parker, could we detour by to see him? Or would it be too dangerous?" Jayde's eyebrows tented together in concern.

"If he can identify Tristan, he might already be in danger. At least I can send protection for him if we know for sure." Caldwell's long stride paused. "In fact, let's go now."

"The cottage can wait, I guess." Jayde looked around. "I sure don't want to see Mr. Pierce in any danger."

They made it to the assisted-living center quickly, the familiar receptionist greeting them as they entered.

"We're here to visit Mr. Pierce," Caldwell explained.

The look on the receptionist's face clouded a bit. "Okay, but I want to warn you. He isn't doing so well today."

"What do you mean?" Jayde asked politely.

"The dementia has been especially bad today. I'm not sure he'll know you." It was obvious from her expression that she thought a great deal of Mr. Pierce. "He didn't know any of us earlier."

Caldwell nodded, a sympathy edging his words as he

replied. "We'll be gentle with him. And if it's too much for him, we'll leave."

When the receptionist nodded, they made their way down the hall to the room Mr. Pierce occupied. "This might not help anything." Caldwell spoke quietly, hoping not to be overheard.

A knock on the door received no answer, and after a moment, Caldwell knocked again before easing the door open.

Mr. Pierce sat near the window, gazing out sightlessly into the lawn beyond. He didn't even turn when they entered.

"Mr. Pierce? How're you feeling today?" Jayde spoke gently from beside him.

He turned at last. "Sadie, I'm hungry. When will dinner be ready?"

Jayde cringed. Looking back at Caldwell, she shrugged. "It's no use, is it?"

Caldwell eased closer. "No. I don't think so. But maybe we can be a comfort to him somehow."

Jayde took up his cue. She leaned closer to Mr. Pierce. "Dinner is soon. What will you do until then?"

His expression changed. "You're not Sadie."

Jayde sat down across from him slowly. "No. I'm not Sadie. Do you remember who I am?"

He squeezed his eyes shut. "No. I can't remember anything these days. I'm sorry. I'm so sorry."

He began to shake his head in despair, and Jayde's heart went out to him. "It doesn't matter. Just know that I'm a friend. What can I do to help you?"

"The Bible. Will you read to me from the Bible?" His searching eyes latched on to hers, and she could only nod in acquiescence. She wouldn't have denied the man any request just then.

She and Caldwell took turns reading to him from the Bible for over half an hour, until a young woman entered with a dinner tray. "I'm sorry, I didn't know he had guests. Would you like to have dinner with Mr. Pierce?"

Jayde and Caldwell exchanged a look before she shook her head. "No, but thank you. I think we had best be going today."

Once they had gone, Caldwell grasped her hand. "I'm sorry for how that worked out. But that was very kind of you."

Jayde's eyes filled with tears. "Not at all. I wish I could do more."

Before they could make it to the hospital, Amelia texted to let them know she and Parker were headed home, so Jayde and Caldwell also returned to Deadman's Cay. Leaving the dock after jetting back to the island, Caldwell and Jayde walked the rest of the way to the cottage in silence. He didn't have to wonder what she was thinking. She seemed as saddened by Mr. Pierce's condition as he was. She hadn't said much at all the whole way home, but her sudden intake of breath as she crossed the threshold of the cottage told him it was still nearly as much of a shock today as it had been yesterday.

"We'll start on cleanup soon. But let's finish checking out the attic first." Caldwell kept one hand on his gun. In all likelihood, the intruder would return to try to find whatever he had been looking for.

Was that why Tristan had been here? Was he behind the whole thing?

If he was, Caldwell would have to tread very carefully. A man willing to attack and kill his own cousins was a very dangerous man indeed.

A sudden thought crossed his mind. If Tristan was a largely successful businessman as Jayde thought, why would he be so desperate to find an expensive diamond? Maybe for fame's sake, but that wasn't a strong enough motive to kill. Caldwell needed to know what Tristan's finances really looked like.

And he knew the quickest way to find out.

An uncomfortable feeling settled in his stomach, but he ignored it. When they reached the attic, he checked it out before letting Jayde inside. Then he did something he once would have sworn he would never do again.

He called his brother Avery.

Jayde sensed something was going on when Caldwell ducked back out of the attic with some vague explanation about needing to make a phone call. When he was gone for several minutes, she knew it must be something significant.

At first, she had thought he was simply calling the museum, since he still hadn't received a response to his email. But then she heard his raised voice. Caldwell rarely raised his voice.

By the time he returned, she was more than a little concerned. His face was a bit flushed, and he didn't look her directly in the eye.

"Is everything okay?" Jayde knew it wasn't. But would he tell her what was going on?

He surprised her by pacing back and forth across the narrow attic. "Yes. No. I'm not really sure."

Clearly something was wrong. "You're not really sure you want to tell me?"

He sat down on top of a storage box with a sigh. "You're right. You deserve to know. I just… Well, it's a long story."

Jayde settled on a box beside him. "I'm listening." She laid a hand over one of his own that lay perched atop one knee. "If you *want* to talk about it. I understand if you don't want to, though."

He put his head in his other hand, long hair curtaining about his chiseled face. "I called Avery. He's my brother. But I haven't talked to him in years."

When he stopped, she simply waited. Obviously there was more to the story.

He took a deep breath before he continued. "My mother left us with my father when I was young. My older brothers practically raised Avery and me. We grew up on a ranch, so we learned to work hard, be tough and ignore our feelings. It created what one of my brothers calls a 'hero complex' in all of us. I tried to run from it. I went to law school and tried to avoid that side of protecting citizens. But I couldn't do it. As you can see, I ended up with a badge and a gun, protecting and serving, just like the rest of the family."

"Nothing wrong with that." Jayde wanted to know the rest of the story now.

"So a few years back, my mother came back around wanting all of us to just forgive and forget. She claimed she'd left because of a prescription drug addiction she was trying to overcome. I couldn't do it, though. I couldn't just forgive her and act like nothing ever happened. My brothers didn't understand why I wouldn't just let it go, but I didn't have it in me." Caldwell looked up at her, blinking back moisture in his eyes. "I grew up without a mother because she left."

"Your father never remarried?"

"No, he wasn't the kind of man to get out and meet anyone when there was work to be done on the ranch." Caldwell shook his head.

"He didn't want to. He never got over her, did he?"

"Who can say? We Thorpe men always hide our feelings, remember? Maybe he missed her. Maybe he was just too hurt by her leaving to ever try again. Well, by the time she came back around, he had already passed away. She made some excuses about leaving out of love and for the sake of our well-being, and all my brothers just welcomed her back in with open arms." He squeezed his eyes shut.

"I understand why you couldn't. You needed more than that from the woman who abandoned you." She felt the sting of tears in her own eyes.

He sat up and wiped the tear from the corner of her eye. "I know my dad loved me. I know my brothers do, too. But there is a void left inside of you when you need a mother's love and she can't give it. Avery just wanted it so badly he was willing to accept it no matter what. He couldn't understand why I turned my back on her."

"But I'm sure you felt that she had turned her back on you." She blinked at the moisture still filling her eyes.

"Yeah. Avery and I argued. He called me selfish for not forgiving her. I suppose some dark, ugly part of me wanted her to pay for leaving us. Avery felt it was his duty to remind me what the Bible says about forgiving. I told him the Old Testament said offenses should be paid 'an eye for an eye,' also. And of course things turned nasty. Our argument actually ended up causing a rift between all my brothers and me."

Jayde covered her mouth with a slender hand for just a second. "So what was so important that you would call him now, after all that?"

She wanted to know if he had changed his mind, but she didn't feel she had the right to ask.

"I've been thinking a lot recently about trying to make amends. With all of them. But until I could find Natalie's killer and completely exonerate myself, I felt like I should wait. Getting a look at financials for your cousin Tristan seemed like a worthy excuse, though. You see, Avery's a private investigator. He could've gotten the information for me in the blink of an eye." Caldwell lowered his head into his hands once more.

"Could have?" Jayde wasn't following that remark.

"I didn't ask him. We argued again, and I…well, I couldn't bring myself to ask for a favor. He asked if I'd forgiven our mother, and I couldn't tell him I had."

"Can I ask you a serious question?" Jayde wasn't sure she wanted to, but she felt the Lord prodding her to do so.

He looked up at her. "Ask away. This can't look much worse on me right now."

She smiled. "What would it take for you to forgive your mother?"

He stared back at her, just a little shocked. "Um, I don't really know. I never really thought about it that way."

"She asked for your forgiveness?" Jayde reached for his hand once more, gently running her hand over his strong fingers.

"Yes. I guess she did." He stared at their hands.

"Do you believe she was sincerely sorry for leaving you? Repentant for it?" Jayde looked down at their hands, as well.

"I suppose so. She didn't seem to have any other motive."

She thought he might be squirming just a bit now.

"What more can she do? She's only human, like the rest of us. We all make mistakes. We all 'sin,' if you will. But God is willing to forgive us. He extends so much grace. Maybe a little grace toward your mother could help you both heal." She let go of his hand then and stood.

He looked up at her, rubbing his hand where hers had

just been. "I know you're right. It's just not easy. But I'll try. I'll definitely try."

She smiled. "Good. Now come look at what I found."

She pushed on a wood panel on the wall behind her, and it swung open, revealing an opening large enough for two people to walk into, and a small chest that looked like a miniature steamer trunk was sitting in the space.

He sucked in a breath, family issues momentarily forgotten.

"You found Natalie's hidden room."

THIRTEEN

"Let's see what's in the box." Jayde motioned for him to reach for it. "I hope it isn't locked."

"If you don't mind, let's take it into the art studio where we have more room and light." Caldwell swallowed hard before reaching for it.

Jayde agreed, and they took the chest to one of the tables, which Jayde cleared off so Caldwell could set it down.

Their eyes met for just a moment as Caldwell placed his hand on the latch. He took a deep breath, hoping she couldn't see him shaking. "Here goes."

The latch opened smoothly, and there in the shadows cast from the lid of the velvet-lined box lay a black drawstring bag of some type of satiny cloth. "What's that?"

Jayde's eyes widened more than they had already. Her breathing quickened. She leaned in close to him, and he caught a whiff of a sweet, floral perfume. Soft, just like Jayde. Delicate.

He forced his attention back to the contents of the chest. His heart sped up in rhythm. It couldn't really be what it looked like, could it?

"You open it." He held it up to Jayde. It was solid and heavy. No way. She couldn't have found it.

But as Jayde slid the strings of the drawstring bag apart and let it fall into her hand, Caldwell could only shake his head in disbelief. "Surely it isn't real."

"Maybe not. We'll have to have it assessed by a professional to know for sure." Jayde held the large stone up to the light. It was over half the size of her fist and sparkled so that it sent tiny twinkles shimmering all over the roof of the sunlit room.

"It isn't as pink as I expected." Caldwell squinted at the gem. It was very pale in color—just a hint of delicate rose.

The hair on the nape of his neck prickled to attention just before a quiet click sounded somewhere below.

"Was that—" But Jayde was already stuffing the stone back into the drawstring bag.

There was a sound in the stairwell, and Caldwell drew his gun, stepping between Jayde and the door.

He heard the chest snap shut, and he motioned for her to take it toward the attic entrance in the bathroom. He hoped she understood what he was trying to tell her, but he couldn't take his eyes off the door in order to make sure. Her light footsteps behind him were the only reassurance he had.

A split second later, the frame of a large man filled the doorway.

"Whoa, hey, Sheriff Thorpe. No need to point a gun at me." His hands went up in surrender.

"Deputy Siebert, what are you doing here?" Caldwell didn't immediately lower the gun. Instead he kept his eyes trained on the newcomer and waited.

His eyes flickered around the room, taking in the scene. "Deputy O'Connor sent me to check on you."

Caldwell slowly lowered the gun. He wasn't sure he believed the story about Ty sending him. "And you couldn't knock on the door before sneaking in? You can understand why I might be cautious." He gestured around the room.

"I knocked, but I guess you didn't hear. Uh, yeah. Ty said your place was wrecked, but this is worse than I expected. Any idea why?" Andrew Siebert was still searching the room with his gaze.

"I have one or two." Was Siebert just trying to back up his story by making it sound like he had talked to Ty?

When Caldwell failed to elaborate, Siebert decided to try another tactic. "Did your visitor leave? The redhead?"

Something in his manner didn't sit well with Caldwell. He studied the man for a moment. "No."

He could see the frustration Siebert was trying to hide as he stepped on into the room. "Was this your wife's art studio? I heard she was quite talented."

Perhaps the man thought flattery might persuade Caldwell to open up. He was wrong.

"Yes, on both counts."

When Caldwell simply continued to stare at him, Siebert began to walk around the room, peering down at partially destroyed canvases as he went. "Would you like me to help you begin some cleanup? This has to be driving you to distraction."

"Thank you, but no. Is there something else you needed, Deputy?"

Andrew Siebert had stopped beside the canvas Natalie had painted of the cove where her body was found. He was staring at it, a look of something akin to unease flitting over his too-handsome features. He masked it quickly, but Caldwell's suspicions had already been aroused.

By the time Siebert looked back at Caldwell, he had schooled his features into a bored expression. But

Caldwell knew that Andrew was aware of his observation. For a brief moment, Andrew Siebert's honest reaction to seeing the painting had been obvious.

"No," he finally replied, his tone seeming intentionally light. "I was just here for you."

But there was a coldness to his words, maybe even an underlying hint of warning. Caldwell was tempted to question him, but he knew it would do no good. Whatever it was that Siebert knew, and however he was involved, he would show his hand eventually.

"Then you're dismissed, Deputy. Get back to work."

Caldwell stared at him until Siebert finally conceded with a nod and made his way to the door. He followed the deputy down the stairs and made sure he left.

Earlier this morning, Caldwell would have been almost certain Tristan Vaughn had been behind the recent attacks. Now he wasn't so sure at all. He wasn't certain Andrew Siebert was, either, but he did heartily believe both men knew more than they were letting on.

Jayde appeared on the stairs when Caldwell didn't come back up. "What was that about?"

"One of my deputies supposedly came to check on me. I think he was up to something. I'm not saying he killed Natalie, or he's covering for whoever did, but he's definitely behaving suspiciously." He glanced out the window, making sure the man didn't return.

Jayde hugged her arms around herself. "What do we do, then?"

"Wait. He'll slip up, I'm sure." Caldwell checked the safety on his gun once more before securely holstering it.

"And the stone?" Jayde's voice shook just a little.

He looked at her, brows drawn. "Leave it where we found it. If no one else has discovered it by now, we have to trust that it's safe there until we figure this out."

Caldwell had an unexplainable suspicion that Andrew Siebert knew what they had just found, and he would be coming for it.

When he did, Caldwell would be waiting.

Jayde wasn't sure what had just transpired, or what was happening inside Caldwell's thoughts, but his manner alone would be terrifying if she didn't know him. He was tense all over, veins standing out along his neck, and his flushed features were solid as granite.

She quietly replaced the stone in Natalie's hidden room, adding the compass and log, as well. Should her cousin be somehow involved in the attacks, he might remember the attic entrance, but she doubted he knew about the hidden room inside the attic. He had stayed at Rose Gem Cottage fewer times than she had growing up, and she hadn't had a clue about the room herself.

Returning to the living room below, she found Caldwell on the phone. The expression on his face was one she had never seen before. She could only describe it as hopeful and relieved.

Not wanting to intrude on whatever significant conversation Caldwell was having, Jayde tried to turn and go back up the stairs, but Caldwell caught her attention with the waving of a hand and then gestured for her to stay.

The waiting mess in the living room made it impossible to sit, and she wasn't sure if the deputies had processed the scene, so she remained standing, hands clasped behind her, and looked out a far window at the beach beyond.

His next words brought her attention to an immediate focus when he spoke them into the phone. "I appreciate that, Avery. I want you to know I'm doing my best. Sometimes forgiveness is difficult, not because you don't want to forgive, but because it still hurts and forgiving somehow feels like betraying your own pain."

He paused for a moment, listening. "You're right. You're still my brothers, and I still love you all. But I understand if you don't want me in your life anymore."

A dejected expression took over his face. "Okay. Well, thanks for doing me this favor, anyway."

He disconnected and sighed.

"Your brother again?" Jayde didn't know where to begin, or if he even wanted to talk about it.

"Yes. He called me back. Said I must've had a very important reason if I swallowed my pride to call him. He's going to find out what Tristan Vaughn's finances look like for us." He shoved his long hair back from his forehead with a sun-browned hand.

"But he doesn't want to make amends." She winced as she stated the obvious. It sounded harsh, though, even to her.

He looked at the ground. "He said he'd like to, but he needs time to process. Maybe he will come around."

"I'm sure he will." Jayde stepped closer to him.

He met her halfway across the room. "Let's go get some food. Then we should be able to think a little more clearly."

The day was warm and humid, especially for fall, but Jayde loved the tropical climate. She would love being here if not for the circumstances. And the attacks.

She missed Natalie, but she had to acknowledge that they hadn't restored their relationship as much as Jayde would have liked before Natalie's death. Perhaps that was the real reason behind her need to find her cousin's killer. She felt she should have kept up their relationship so maybe Natalie would have confided in her. It might have kept her alive.

The wedge between them had begun with Dylan Chambers, a serious boyfriend in Jayde's past, a man who had turned out to be controlling and narcissistic. But Jayde had believed herself to be in love, despite the early signs. Natalie had warned Jayde that Dylan wasn't good for her. Natalie had always had a knack for reading people. But Jayde hadn't wanted to believe her, and as the relationship grew more serious, the cousins had argued about it more frequently, leading to eventual loss of contact altogether.

Jayde eventually saw through Dylan when she caught him talking to another woman behind her back, but it was years later, and he had managed to alienate her from most of her friends and family by then. He tried manipulating her into getting back together and getting married more than once, she believed because of her family's money, but Jayde had finally gotten her own two strong legs beneath her and used her head. She struggled to trust another man after that, however.

It was never the same between her and Natalie, though. They had only started talking again a few short months before Natalie's death.

And Jayde hadn't dated since.

She truly hadn't wanted to until recently. It didn't escape her notice that irony played a role in it being Caldwell Thorpe who made her want to change her mind. She certainly hadn't seen that coming.

Almost as if he had read her thoughts, Caldwell spoke, breaking into her musings. "I feel like maybe you know a little something about what I'm dealing with concerning my family."

Jayde sighed. "You're aware that Natalie and I had grown distant with one another by the time the two of you married."

Caldwell nodded. "She only told me your boyfriend was trouble and that's why she had tried to help you see that. She said it caused problems between the two of you."

Jayde slowed her pace as they walked. "She was right, though. Dylan was only in it for himself. The relationship, life, everything. He was so self-absorbed that he was willing to shower me with flattery and gifts to distract me from the fact that he didn't really love me. But he saw my family's wealth and my success and thought he'd have the life he had always dreamed of if he could land me as his wife."

Caldwell grunted. "Sounds like a real jerk."

Jayde laughed. "He was. I don't know why I didn't see it sooner. He became demanding and verbally abusive when I tried to break it off. He was manipulative. A bit scary sometimes, really. I was glad to finally be free of him."

"I'm glad you're free of him, also. I'm sorry you went through that, though." He grasped her hand as she paused before picking up the pace again.

His tender gesture sent warmth that had nothing to do with the tropical climate surging through her. When he released her hand, she longed for his touch to return.

Her thoughts were soon diverted from the man beside her when she felt, rather than saw, a shadow following them at a distance. They were being watched.

She thought Caldwell noticed about the same time, for he reached for her hand again and gave it a slight squeeze. Jayde stepped a little closer to him, waiting for any signal. He kept walking along like nothing was wrong for a couple more minutes. She felt safer just having him grip her hand.

But looking around, she really didn't know where they could go if anyone came at them. It was just an empty sidewalk with beachfront homes here and there. What few stores there were on the island were farther down. And she didn't want to put anyone in danger. But there was nowhere on this island to hide.

Her pulse picked up speed, and she knew they were running out of time. Whoever was following them was about to make their move.

"Run!"

Caldwell's voice was a stage whisper, but he launched into a sprint at the same time, dragging her along by the hand. She didn't have time to look back, but she could hear another set of shoes pounding against the sidewalk behind them.

She pushed herself with all her might, but Caldwell's legs were much longer than her own and he soon pulled ahead, tugging at her hand. She tried to let go, so he slowed a little and gripped it more tightly. Her muscles and lungs both began to burn in protest. She kept up the pace as long as she could, but before they could reach safety, she began to feel herself slowing down. A hand clamped down on her upper arm and yanked her fiercely from Caldwell's clasp.

She shrieked at the brutal assault, but before Caldwell could react, she felt the cold press of steel against her temple. She couldn't hold back one last whimper, but then she fell silent.

From the corner of her eye, she could see that her assailant wore black from head to toe—long-sleeved shirt, pants, gloves and shoes. A solid black bandana was tied around his head like a ninja, and he wore dark glasses.

Caldwell had turned to come after Jayde and her attacker, but he skidded to a stop, fury mottling his face at the sight of the SIG held against her head. She could feel herself trembling, even as her lungs still fought to take in enough oxygen. Her attacker, also, was breathing hard.

"Where's the stone?" His deep voice sounded almost falsely so. Was he afraid of revealing his identity?

"I don't know what stone you're talking about." Caldwell issued the cool reply as he stared the man down, unblinking.

Jayde's assailant tightened his hold on her. "You sure about that? I think you're lying. Where's the diamond?"

Caldwell's jaw clenched visibly. "Let her go."

The black-clad figure shook his head. "Not happening. You can either give me what I want, or I take her hostage."

"To where? There's nowhere on this island for you to go. No escape. Even with a hostage you're still trapped." Caldwell didn't move a muscle as he attempted to negotiate.

Jayde was sure Caldwell knew how to handle a hostage situation, but she desperately wished he would hurry. The nose of the SIG against her skin was trembling. Would he slip? What if he accidentally shot her? Or grew angry and tired of waiting?

"This is awfully bold of you, out here in the open in broad daylight, on an island where you can't run far without a boat." Caldwell's tone was almost lazy.

"What makes you think I don't have one?"

Jayde sincerely hoped not.

But he didn't make any move to drag her toward the water. In fact, he didn't make any move to drag her anywhere. She had no idea what to make of that.

"Because you'd be trying a lot harder to get there." Caldwell still didn't so much as flinch.

"Listen, I'm the one with the gun. I'm making the calls here. So lay your own weapon on the ground very slowly.

Then put your hands in the air and start walking." Her attacker jerked her up higher in his grasp.

Caldwell started doing as he said, but he still asked the question. "To where? There's nowhere for me to go."

"Yes, there is. That house up there is empty and there's a storage building out behind it. Head there."

He was planning to lock Caldwell in a random storage building? And then what? Where would he take her?

"Okay, I'm moving." But as he laid the gun on the ground, she thought she saw his thumb slide up the back of his hand while her attacker was looking away. Her eyes lingered there for a second, even as he rose to his feet again. The sunlight gave a tiny blip of reflection off his smartwatch, and she realized what he had done. He had made an emergency call.

He raised both hands over his head then and started walking. Jayde's attacker pushed her along behind him. Jayde could smell sweat and some sort of soured fabric softener smell coming off the man holding the gun on her. He was too close. She felt like his breath was pushing at her hair on the back of her head, and it made her cringe. She heard his shuffling footsteps kicking sand, and it hit her ankles in a rude spray of grit with every step. Where was the response to Caldwell's call?

They kept walking until they were almost to the storage building. Jayde felt the adrenaline surge as her captor was about to force Caldwell into the building. It was going to be too late.

But just in time, the sound of sirens reached them. Two patrol cars were pulling up, she could see from the corner of her eye. She didn't dare move her head.

He shoved her around to face the deputies, but when four of them stepped out of the vehicles, he panicked and abandoned his plan altogether.

With a vicious shove, he pushed her away and fled.

She shrieked and watched as Caldwell surged after him, fighting to get enough power in the deep sand to gain on him. He lunged to tackle him, and both men hit the ground, rolling on the beach in a struggle that had Jayde yelling for the officers to hurry.

Her captor wasn't as strong as Caldwell, and he had to work harder to evade Caldwell's grip. He squirmed and writhed but never quite broke loose. His sunglasses fell off in the struggle and Jayde gasped, startling him into going still just long enough for Caldwell to gain the upper hand. When he had him face down in the sand and the officers were cuffing his wrists, Caldwell looked up to see why she had sounded so surprised. Recognition flooded him, as well, once he finally got a good look at the eyes peering out at them from between the black bandanas above and below them.

It was her cousin Tristan.

FOURTEEN

Caldwell had suspected his involvement but realizing Tristan Vaughn had tried to kidnap his own cousin just filled him with disgust. What was wrong with this guy? Was he so desperate for money that he had to resort to such base measures?

Crouching beside him, he looked him in the eye. He pulled the cloth from the lower part of his face, exposing Tristan's mouth set in a rigid line. In a hard voice he scarcely used, Caldwell asked the question that troubled him most. "Did you kill Natalie?"

Tristan only glared at him from the sand. "I know my rights."

He said no more, and fury gnawed at Caldwell. He wanted to lash out somehow, but he knew it would do no good. He would only be in trouble for assaulting a suspect.

Reluctantly, Caldwell gave him over to the deputies, Ty among them. "Get him to a holding cell and call his lawyer. You should have his number from last time."

Jayde stood a few yards away with her arms wrapped around her waist, another deputy standing guard beside her. She looked so betrayed, he ached for her. She had admitted she and her cousin hadn't been close, but he was still family. It was a terrible blow, in any case.

They accompanied the deputies to the department with the suspect, where his lawyer was soon present via video call. He advised his client not to speak, of course, and Tristan didn't.

Jayde peered at him through shatterproof glass, shaking her head sadly. "What is it about the love of money that can turn people so? We were never close, but I had no idea Tristan could be so evil."

Caldwell took her hand. "I'm sorry this happened. I wish I could explain it for you, but I don't understand it, either."

With one last shake of her head, Jayde turned away from Tristan. "It's going to be hard on his parents. They are getting on in years."

Caldwell pushed back his hair. He wanted to get her mind off of such humbling thoughts. "Let's get back to the cottage. There's nothing to gain from being here right now."

They barely spoke until they got there, but the destruction remaining reminded them both of so many questions they needed answers to, and by the time they got into the house, Jayde seemed close to tears. He hadn't done a very good job of redirecting her thoughts.

"How did he know we found it?" She walked around the room. "Do you think he was here? Was he spying on us from inside the house the whole time?"

She shivered, and he reassured her. "No, surely not. I always check to be sure no one is in the house. It had to be another way."

She walked up the stairs and he followed. "What are you doing?"

"Just looking." She had that determined air about her once more.

Jayde continued, making her way around the studio, and looking carefully at everything. She moved piles of paints and papers and canvases. Finally, she paused as she unearthed a small box with a tiny eye, barely peeking out at the room. It was some sort of video camera.

She held it up. "Does this belong to you?"

Fury surged up in him anew. How could he have missed this? "Of course it doesn't. How did we miss it? I'll take it in."

Her expression was full of questions, but she didn't ask. Maybe he looked as furious as he felt. He took a deep breath. His anger wasn't going to help them. He had to get control of it.

"It can likely be traced. It will take a while, but the feed has to be going somewhere. Tristan was probably counting on us being dead before it was discovered." He probably shouldn't be so blunt with her, but her cousin had already spelled it all out for them.

"So we have something on him now, right? Does that mean they can keep him locked up this time?" She was pale and kept shivering. Sympathy flooded him for the shock she was likely enduring. And he still hadn't even been able to get her anything to eat.

"No, I'm afraid not. Not unless they can trace it back to him somehow. That's why I want to take it in." Caldwell's voice had softened. He had turned off the camera and was now examining it closely.

"What about the diamond? And the other artifacts?" She sounded a little disgusted just mentioning the cause of all this.

He was considering the angle the camera had been facing. It had been looking toward the table, but not the attic door. It had faced away in the opposite direction. So most likely he had seen them unearth the diamond from the chest while it was sitting on the table, but he hadn't been able to see where Jayde had taken it after placing it back in the chest.

"We'll take them to the museum once we get all this worked out." He didn't want to worry about the stone right now any more than she did. He just wanted it over, for her sake. She seemed so fragile right now, it made his chest ache.

"Should you take them to the sheriff's department and lock them up? Or should we just hide it somewhere else?" She looked around the room. "If they can't press any charges, he could come back, right?"

Caldwell thought for a moment. "Let's hope that doesn't happen. But we'll take them and lock them in the safe just to be sure. I should have done that before. I just thought that it might be safer to leave it all here, since he's been watching our every move."

"Is it safe to move it now?" Jayde's wide green eyes moved to the window and peered outside.

"As long as he's still in custody. Just to be cautious, I'll take it tonight when there's no one about. I'll have a couple of deputies come and accompany me."

"You believe they are trustworthy?" She wasn't questioning his opinion, but reassuring herself, he decided, seeing her anxious expression.

"Yes. I do." But his mind drifted to Andrew Siebert and all of his questions. For some reason, he didn't want the man to know anything about the whereabouts of the diamond. "I'll make sure to choose men I know I can trust."

Andrew Siebert was not one of those men, even if he wasn't the one in custody right now. He might not be involved, but he wasn't someone Caldwell trusted with something this big, for sure.

He didn't want her worrying, so he changed the topic of conversation. "I promised you food earlier. Let's get something to eat before they call me back to the station."

While she was nodding, however, his thoughts went to how vulnerable she looked standing there in the middle of the ransacked studio. He had a sudden urge to just get rid of this place and move back home to Wyoming. And when he pictured doing that, she was right there by his side. It shook him up. What was going on with him?

"Caldwell? Are you okay?" She placed a hand on his upper arm as she asked it, and he was touched by her tender concern. He should be asking her the same thing.

"Yes. I was just thinking maybe after I clean this place up, I should just give it to your parents. It doesn't seem it was meant to be mine. I've got too many unhappy memories here." He spoke without thought, but something in Jayde's expression made him wonder if he had offended her somehow.

"I just meant, with Natalie. Her death. And all this trouble with the diamond."

She turned away, and he had the odd feeling he hadn't helped things at all with his rambling explanation. "I knew what you meant."

Her voice sounded a little hollow, though.

He stepped closer to her. "Did I say something wrong?"

She turned back around, and he found they were suddenly far too close together. He could smell her sweet perfume and feel the warmth from her body.

She looked as surprised as he felt, but then she leaned in and gently laid her soft, full lips against his own. It was the sweetest, most amazing thing he had ever felt.

He closed his eyes and leaned in as she wrapped her arms around him. She felt wonderfully soft, and he stood there wondering how he had ever deserved to feel something like this.

Until she pulled away, and the coolness of the air conditioning rushed in between them, reminding him of where they were and why.

Her eyes shuttered, and he realized his own arms still hung close to his sides in surprise. Had she thought he was rejecting her kiss?

"I'm sorry, Caldwell. I know I shouldn't have. You're Natalie's husband." She tried to smile. "She always did get the best guys."

He was shaking his head. "Don't be sorry. I've wanted to do that a time or two myself."

"Really?" The need for reassurance was evident, in her tone, her expression and the way she tilted her head in question, as well.

"Really." He put as much meaning as he could into that one word. He didn't reach for her, though he wanted to kiss her again and more thoroughly this time. "And I might have been Natalie's husband. But she's no longer here. We can't change that."

"That may be. But she won your heart." Jayde lowered her head.

"It isn't a secret we had relationship problems before Natalie died. I loved her. But that's all in the past. I don't want to talk about Natalie." Caldwell gently lifted her face to see her eyes.

"I'm sorry I mentioned it." Jayde looked immensely sad.

"Don't be sorry for that, either. But I do want to put it all behind me and move on. I never expected to feel these emotions again. I don't know if I'm ready to feel them. I will never be sorry you kissed me, though."

He leaned toward her and raised his brows at her. She actually smiled then.

He thought his returned grin probably said more than his words possibly could have.

Jayde's emotions were in such turmoil that she wanted to run.

She wouldn't, though. Even if just seeing Caldwell's expression set her pulse careening off at the visions of her most romantic daydreams it conjured up.

No matter what he said, she couldn't replace Natalie. He had loved her first. What if he always loved her more? Not that he had said anything about loving her, but she wouldn't enter into any romantic relationship if she thought there wasn't a possibility of love developing. And in Caldwell's case, if it did, would she always be competing with Natalie's memory?

She couldn't take the risk. Her heart was too fragile. She couldn't be content with taking second place to a memory. It would break her heart, and the best way to avoid that happening was to not let herself fall in love with Caldwell.

But she was afraid she already had.

"No worries." She tried for a confident tone. "I don't know if I'm ready, either. We might as well pretend it never happened."

"Whoa, whoa, wait a minute." Caldwell narrowed his eyes at her. "I didn't say that. I don't think I'll be forgetting that kiss for a while, so pretending it never happened is out of the question if you ask me."

"Fine. But it won't happen again." She drew herself

up and fortified her posture with a bracing breath. "Let's take care of those valuables."

For a moment, she thought Caldwell might argue, but he let it go. He went into the other room and began making some calls, from what she could hear.

Jayde's thoughts turned to his declaration that he wanted to be rid of the cottage. Did that mean the whole island, or just the beach cottage? And where did he plan to go?

She hadn't meant to react when he had mentioned the bad memories, but it had felt a little personal after everything they had been through together in the past few days. She didn't know why, exactly, because even the majority of her own memories of the island were still filled with Natalie and the time they spent here as children. How could she begrudge him having the same problem? And maybe in time, it wouldn't be so difficult for either of them. Perhaps one day they could enjoy the island without memories of tragedy cropping into their thoughts as they did now.

But again, she was envisioning her own future with Caldwell's, and soon she would tell him goodbye and never see him again. Why did that thought hurt so much?

She had a job and a life to get back to, really. Maybe not a very exciting life, but she had friends and a career. But since spending the last few days with Caldwell, being in danger but still being close to him in so many ways, she had not only softened toward him.

She had fallen in love with him.

It was pointless to pretend otherwise. She couldn't act on those tender feelings, of course, but she really couldn't deny them, either. It was going to hurt. It would take time. But she would have to move on and forget him.

Because even if he returned her feelings, Jayde just didn't know if she could ever believe in love that much.

She wasn't meant for the fairy tale.

Her thoughts drifted to what he had said about his relationship with Natalie. Jayde knew from experience that Natalie could be somewhat difficult at times. She tended to be a bit dramatic, and often very spoiled. But Jayde had loved her cousin and just accepted it all as a part of who Natalie was, even if it had been hard for Jayde to understand at times.

Jayde considered their family relationships. Natalie's father, Phillip, and Jayde's mother, Anastasia, were siblings, as well as Tristan's mother, Felicity, and though they often vacationed together and of course got together on holidays, there had always been a certain tension among the siblings. There were many times Jayde had felt her mother didn't really want to be around her family, but Jayde hadn't really understood why.

Snippets of things Tristan had said came floating back to her. When he had mentioned her mother's frequent fights with her father, it had reminded her of the questions she had had about it earlier. Maybe she should take Caldwell's advice and ask her mother for the full story on why she hadn't gotten along well with her father and siblings.

It was time Jayde knew the truth.

FIFTEEN

Caldwell made arrangements with a few of the deputies to help with the relocation of the diamond and the artifacts, and they came up with a plan. He was still working on the small things when his phone rang.

"Sheriff Thorpe." He didn't look at the number before answering. He had gotten out of the habit since so many calls he received were from those not listed in his contacts, anyway.

Avery's voice on the other end surprised him. "You were right about Vaughn. The man is in some big trouble with his finances. Looks like he put it all in some stocks before the recent market downturn and hasn't recovered. His business is nearing bankruptcy."

"Of course. We have him in custody currently for attempted kidnapping. But I don't have enough on him to charge him with the murder yet. Any thoughts?" Caldwell tried to keep his tone light, as if there had never been any problems between them.

"He made it look like an accident, right? I don't know if there's any way you could find proof that he somehow capsized her boat. Might have to take another route. He needs to confess." Avery cleared his throat. "Look, we're all on our way to the island. I talked to Beau, Briggs and Grayson, and we all think it's time we sat down and talked this thing out. Are you good with that?"

Caldwell let out a relieved breath. "Of course I'm good with that. When are you coming down?"

"Soon. Maybe this evening. As quickly as we can get flights."

"Why the hurry?" Caldwell heard a touch of laughter in his own voice. "Not that I mind."

"I'll explain when we get there."

Avery disconnected and left Caldwell pondering what he meant. Was everything okay?

He would just have to find out when they got here, he supposed. Right now he had to finish preparing the artifacts and find out who to contact at the museum. He was ready to be free of this diamond and pirate treasure business.

Jayde helped him get it all situated for transport, wrapped carefully in newspaper and packed into sealed boxes. Still, the thought of traveling with such delicate cargo set his nerves a little on edge. Any accidental, reckless move on his part could damage the artifacts beyond repair.

When the deputies arrived, they packed them carefully into the unit and prepared to head out. Jayde waved them off, and he felt a brief pang over their shared kiss. How he would like to lean in and kiss her goodbye before he left. But that wasn't going to happen. He had failed at keeping Natalie safe. He wouldn't get distracted and fail Jayde, too. He had to get this wrapped up and send her home in one piece.

Once they had the artifacts and the diamond concealed in the safe at the sheriff's department, Caldwell felt like he could finally breathe again. Jayde had wanted to begin work on the cottage, so he left her there, promising to check on her frequently. With Tristan in custody, he didn't think they had anything to worry about. He had a deputy posted just in case, but he had a pile of work to catch up on. Hopefully the only help Tristan had had was from hired men.

Caldwell found he couldn't stand to look at Tristan. He turned his back so that he wouldn't have to think about what the man had done to his own cousins, all for the sake of money. The fact that he had lawyered up and wouldn't talk made it worse, leaving Caldwell to have to endure the man's presence that much longer. And he didn't really know if they were going to be able to hold him for the murder if they didn't come up with some proof. Attempted kidnapping wasn't going to cut it as far as charges go. Caldwell wanted to see him pay for what he had done to Natalie.

He all but lost track of time until the sun began to sink in the sky. He considered leaving it for the next day, but between all of the work he needed to catch up on and the diamond sitting in the safe, he felt like he needed to stay. As darkness fell, he had to quell a growing sense of unease. He kept going to check to see that Tristan was still safely locked up in the holding cell.

After a couple of hours, he started hearing things. He thought someone else was in the building, but when he searched, there was no one else there but the deputy in charge of keeping watch over Tristan and Ty O'Connor. He looked out the windows on both sides, but he couldn't see anyone.

Going back to work, he tried to concentrate and ignore his paranoia. He pushed back the nagging thought at the back of his mind that there could have been someone else involved other than the hired gunmen.

What real reason could Andrew Siebert have for being

involved? Was he just suspicious of Andrew because he didn't care for the man personally? There was always money as a motivator, but it just didn't fully explain things. There was something he was missing. Something they still needed to piece together.

To ease his mind, he sent Jayde a text message making sure she was okay. She replied quickly, assuring him she was fine, so he forced his mind back to the matter at hand.

Avery texted him as soon as they got off the plane and Caldwell told him that he was at the station, though Jayde was still at the cottage. He let her know his brothers might come by so it wouldn't surprise her if they showed up there.

He was buried deep in a pile of reports when the door opened and his four brothers marched in, but while Caldwell was about to gather them all for a hug of forgiveness, Avery came at him in a rush.

"Later, kid. Jayde's missing. She's not at the cottage like you thought." He was gesturing wildly. "Let's go."

"I'm driving, though, so if you want shotgun you'd better call it now." Grayson took charge with the remark while Beau approached with a cell phone.

"We found this in the yard back at the cottage." He handed it over. Your deputy's patrol car in the driveway was empty.

"It's hers, isn't it?" Briggs spoke up from the back of the pack, talking about the phone.

"What? No. I can't believe I left her." Caldwell hurried back to check the holding cell where they had Tristan and back at his brothers. "Ty! Where is Deputy Siebert?"

Ty burst through the door next to them. "He's not on duty this evening. Said he was leaving the island for a day or two."

"I knew it." Caldwell shook his head at his own foolishness. "How could I have believed he didn't have anything to do with it? He was in on this all along."

"Explain on the way. Come on," Grayson urged.

Caldwell slammed his palm against the wall, but then he shouted orders at Ty to keep an eye on Tristan and not let him leave before he heard back from him.

The brothers took off at a sprint.

"Any ideas where he would have taken her?" Avery was leading the way back out to the waiting truck.

"The cove. The one where he killed Natalie." He looked around at his brothers. "It'll be faster on foot. You old men think you can keep up?"

If anyone was around to see the five large Thorpe men running down the sidewalk like a posse after an outlaw, they wouldn't have understood the significance of the event.

Caldwell had really missed having brothers.

The waves crashed almost invisibly in the dark night. The moon was hidden behind a thick veil of clouds, and the rise in the landscape hid them from view. Trees surrounded them on the other side, and even in the dark, Jayde knew exactly where he had brought her to.

"Why are you bringing me back to the cove where Natalie was killed?" Jayde knew exactly what Andrew had planned, but she wanted to make him say it.

"Killed? Her death was ruled an accident. Just as yours will be. Now that I have your other dear cousin out of the way, we can get down to business. I'm sure he and Sheriff Thorpe are going to keep each other busy for a while." He smiled but it was full of evil, despite the first impression he gave of being handsome.

"You framed Tristan. Made it look like this was him

when it was you all along." Jayde pulled ceaselessly at the zip ties he had secured around her wrists.

"Oh, Tristan was guilty. But I made it look like he was just using hired thugs, and no one is going to believe we were working together on this. The trouble is, with him in custody, I'm going to have to take extra care to make sure your death looks accidental. I won't be able to pin it on him." Andrew was gazing off into the distance as if he were appreciating his own brilliance. "And he isn't here to mess up the plan. He thought he knew where the stone was. Swore it was safe to go ahead and kill her while the timing was right. He was wrong. He didn't know where the stone was. But you do."

"So that just leaves one problem. If you kill me, how will you find the stone?" Jayde tried to sound confident, but her voice shook.

He laughed, and she found no amusement in the sound. "Oh, there's the fun part. I have something to show you. But first, let me tell you about what I have planned for you. The only question is, do you want to die quickly? Or you can put up a fight and cause me more problems and I will make it slow and painful. By the time I'm finished I will have you begging me to just end it." He shoved her along the beach a little harder than necessary, causing her to stumble in the sand. "You see, you're going to help me trap Thorpe. He knows too much."

Her blood went cold at his mention of harming Caldwell. "And how do you expect me to do that? How will you even know if I'm telling the truth? If I tell you wrong, it will be too late."

He shrugged as if it didn't matter. "Thorpe never suspected me until you came along. He might not have ever liked me, but he didn't suspect I was after the diamond. But he's also going to die. It's only a matter of time…"

"And what if Tristan decides to give you up? He could be telling Sheriff Thorpe everything right now. Maybe they offered him a deal to tell everything he knew." Jayde hoped with everything in her that he would, and soon.

"He won't. He thinks this is all part of the plan. That I would take care of you, dispose of Thorpe, get the diamond and then get the charges against him dropped. He thought we would split the money and go our separate ways as soon as it was safe to do so. But he can rot in prison for all I care. Your grandfather killed mine, double-crossed him and took the diamond. Now I'm going to pay back the favor, just as my mother always wanted." Andrew's eyes were so cold with malice, she couldn't help wondering how long he had been allowing that knowledge to fester inside his heart.

"Your grandfather?" It all began to sink in, and Jayde felt a sickening knot in the pit of her stomach. "He was part of the original partnership to find the diamond, wasn't he?"

Andrew made a disgusted sound. "You mean you really didn't have all that figured out? You're not quite as bright as your dear cousin. Are you?"

"I don't know what you mean."

"Thorpe's wife had it all figured out. I'm surprised you never thought to find out if the man Thurman Farley killed had any relatives."

As full realization set in, Jayde felt her hopes begin to sink.

"My grandfather got greedy. But I'm not my grandfather. We can still split the money from the museum and no one else has to die." She was thinking of Caldwell. If she could convince Andrew to just take half the money and be gone, she would gladly do it.

"It's too late for that. Besides, his traitorous blood

runs in your veins. How could I ever trust you? Not only might you betray me when it came to the money, how do I know you wouldn't tell everything else you know? I don't trust anyone." He twisted her arm brutally to drive home his point. It was barely beginning to heal, and the fire wrenched through her whole frame, producing a pained cry from Jayde.

He pushed her up the beach toward the rocky steps leading up to the cave.

"Why are you bringing me here?" Jayde's voice was high-pitched but insistent.

"I want to show you something before I kill you." His voice was full of triumph.

They approached the cave, and she realized the entrance wasn't underwater right now. The moon was full. High tide would be later tomorrow morning.

He shoved her toward the mouth of the cave, causing her to stumble over the rocks that jutted up around the edges of the sand by its entrance. She gasped as he twisted her arms, the rope he had secured them with biting into her tender wrists. She had lost her sandals in the deep sand and now winced at the sharp rocks pressing into her bare feet. Cool spray from the ocean showered her bare legs beneath her shorts, and a briny smell mixed with the slight tang of fish and seaweed. Ordinarily she would have loved being on the beach at night.

She wasn't sure she would ever feel the same again if she survived this attack.

When they entered the darkness of the cave, Andrew fumbled with one hand for a moment before turning on a small flashlight he had stashed in a pocket. After shoving her farther in, he aimed it carefully, and when the beam fell on the diamond and the other artifacts lying on the cloth they had been carefully wrapped in, she couldn't contain her gasp.

"How did you get those?" Jayde asked.

He shoved her closer, making sure she got a good look.

"It wasn't difficult to break into the county safe. It's not like I haven't had access to it before. And so predictable of Caldwell Thorpe to take it there." With his free hand, he reached out and touched the diamond almost reverently.

She didn't explain to him that he was wrong. That had been Jayde's idea.

"And how do you plan to get away with stealing them when several other deputies knew they were in that vault?" Jayde honestly didn't know the answer to that one.

"It's simple. I'll return them before anyone knows they are gone. I have proof that they should belong to my family. Letters, handwritten by both of our grandfathers, before Farley decided to double-cross my grandfather. My mother kept them all." Andrew sounded so self-satisfied it made a shiver run down her back.

"Okay, then why did you bring them here?" Jayde shook her head. He wasn't making much sense to her.

"A few reasons. I wanted you to see what caused you and your cousin to die, to realize your greedy grandfather ultimately led to your own deaths. But I also wanted Thorpe to know I have been outsmarting him this whole time. I want him to see I was one step ahead of him through the whole adventure. He thinks he's so smart, the high and mighty sheriff. But I talked to Pierce first. I knew what Thorpe's wife was doing first. And I was the first to learn the cottage was full of secrets. There were even more than I first thought. But more than anything, I wanted all of you to pay. I have been planning this whole thing for quite some time. You all fell right into the setup. Isn't it wild that that little rock caused all of this?" He cackled.

"You can at least spare Caldwell. He doesn't know yet, and you can take the diamond and fly off to somewhere in the Caribbean and forget all about this place. But leave Caldwell out of it. He didn't have anything to do with the betrayal between our grandfathers." Jayde couldn't do anything about the tears she felt rolling down her cheeks.

"Aw." Andrew was full of sarcasm. "You're in love with the sheriff. How cute. Would you take your cousin's hand-me-downs so quickly?"

His gibe hit its mark. Jayde swallowed hard. Hadn't she thought something similar herself? But it didn't matter. Even if he was never hers to love, she would do anything to save him. She knew deep in her heart that he would do the same for her. She just didn't know how she was going to save him right now. She had to think fast, or she would be dead before she could. She prayed silently for guidance. She also prayed that God would somehow keep Caldwell safe.

He had jerked her around and began shoving her back out onto the beach. She wanted to cry out, but she wouldn't give him that satisfaction. But she wanted to lash out.

"Better than a man who's too cowardly to make his own way in life." She flung the stinging remark over her shoulder.

She didn't know where the words came from. She wasn't sure if angering him was a good idea, but maybe he would become careless. And it made her feel slightly better.

His reaction was to shove her once again, quite mercilessly this time. She landed on her knees, unable to catch herself with her hands, and narrowly avoided hitting the sand face-first. She managed to get her forearms between her head and the dunes just in time. The impact sent a jolt of pain through her shoulders, especially the one she had recently injured, and the bare skin on her knees and forearms burned from the abrasive sand. She gasped, unable to keep from knocking the breath out of her lungs.

He stood over her, laughing. "You might want to rethink that kind of talk. Besides, I see things differently. I'm making myself rich. I'm taking matters into my own hands. Don't you think I want to see my grandfather's death avenged?"

She couldn't breathe well enough to respond. She raised her eyes to him, though, and focused all her disdain into her stare. "I had nothing to do with your grandfather's death. I wasn't even alive at the time. They were little more than boys."

He ignored her. "What I don't understand, though, is why your grandfather never collected any money for the diamond. Did someone else know his secret? Had my grandfather confided in someone else that your grandfather feared?" Andrew paced back and forth in front of her, hand over his mouth as he thought about it.

"How did you learn about what happened? You had to have heard the story somewhere. Who told you?" She was still struggling to draw a healthy breath, so she gasped out the words.

"I've always known. My mother told me when I was very young. She told me the Rose Stone was real, that the stone was found and the double cross actually happened, but I didn't believe it for a very long time. My family even owned part of the island at one time. But my mother needed the money, so she eventually sold it, and naturally your family ended up with it." He paused to glare at her.

"You knew all along? About the diamond, the double cross, the whole thing?" Jayde still couldn't believe he had known so much. Had her family known, as well?

"Of course I knew. My mother died in poverty. She had cancer and couldn't afford treatments. She might have lived, with treatment, but she wouldn't leave me with the kind of debt it would have taken to make her well. Before her death, she made me promise to get revenge. Do you know how much guilt and anger that left me with? So I came to the island to work and find out where the diamond was, to take back what was ours." He sneered at her.

"But Natalie found it first." Jayde sat back on her heels, filling with sympathy for the circumstances that had brought this man to such a point.

"Don't give me that look. I don't want your pity. She did find it first. And she felt that same pity you're feeling for me now. She wrote me a letter, wanting to make amends. She never mailed it, but I found it when I was looking for the diamond one day before she died. They had left the island to go see her parents one weekend, and I knew where the spare key was hidden. Do you know how disconcerting it was to be rifling through her notes in her studio and see my name staring back at me? Almost like she was expecting me." He started pacing through the heavy sand again.

Clearly he wanted her to know everything. She was grateful, for it gave her time to think of a plan. She wanted to keep him talking.

"What else did the letter say? What did you do with it?"

He snorted. "It said she had found her grandfather's journal, the pink diamond and the artifacts that went along with it, and she wanted to meet and discuss how we could go about sharing the proceeds from the museum for returning it. As if I could be content to share it after all our family had suffered at your hands."

"Do you still have the letter?" Jayde asked the question again. He was too busy spouting disdain for her family and revenge to notice when something caught her eye in the moonlit darkness. Could she have possibly seen people moving low along the beach? Hope surged within her, but she schooled her expression. If he read it on her face it would all be over. He would kill her before anyone could get to them. The shadows were still a good distance away.

"Why would I keep it? I didn't want any reminders of what had happened. I burned it. The journal, too. If anyone found it in my possession, it would have brought my involvement into question. As it was, I didn't have the slightest connection to Natalie Thorpe that anyone knew of. Apparently she never told her fool husband anything. She wrote in the journal that she wanted to surprise him with the Rose Stone, since she didn't think he would believe her. He didn't know about the journal, the double cross, the letter, the diamond, none of it." He grinned, but it looked evil, even though he was handsome. She could see beyond the sculpted features, and his soul was black and rotten from the bitterness he harbored—as black as his hair in the dark night.

"I understand that." She kept her tone neutral. "You must have been devastated to lose your mother. I'm sorry she suffered."

His eyes narrowed. Anger mottled his features. "I don't want your sympathy! You're going to pay either way. I'll make sure you suffer also. Maybe not as long as my mother did, but I'll do what I can with the time we have."

"How did Tristan become involved?" Jayde still wasn't sure how they came to work together. Her cousin seemed to have lied to her about everything.

"Natalie contacted him, as well. She said she wanted everyone to get their share. She was naive enough to think it would work out so easily." He snorted again. "She even told him she was sending me a letter."

"And did you contact him or vice versa?" Jayde didn't really care about every single detail, but it kept him talking—which kept her alive. She was also wondering why Natalie hadn't contacted her, as well, if she wanted everyone to get their share.

"He contacted me, though I don't know why it matters. He probably intended to double-cross me just like his grandfather did with mine. Why else would he have lied about knowing where the diamond was?" His face grew harder in the moonlight.

"Tristan lies about a lot of things." She muttered the words. "Who left the camera in the cottage? Was it you or him?"

He laughed. "Oh, you found that, did you? That was actually my idea. I had him plant it, though. When he couldn't find the diamond, I had him plant it in the mess before he left. It's been there since he searched the cottage."

She took a deep breath. Tristan was here on the island when she had called him, then. He had been the one to ransack the cottage. They had never known he was here until it was too late.

"The boat. Did he attack us or was that you?" She was thinking of the night Caldwell had been called to Key West. The officer had been conveniently found shortly after they survived the attack.

"I was on duty. Made it easy to make sure the sheriff

had to come to Key West. I had one of my men see to it that Mendoza disappeared for a little while. He's a small guy. And then I could 'find' him later. So I sent him to try to kill you then. But it didn't work. Tristan turned out to be a terrible partner in every way, you see. It kept me from feeling too badly when I decided to go ahead and frame him for everything." He shrugged.

A shudder of revulsion rippled through Jayde. He was truly despicable. And all because he wanted revenge.

"But the man who attacked us at the cottage…" She could easily see that Andrew wasn't as large as that man had been. And Tristan certainly wasn't.

"Just some flunky we hired. Learned our lesson fast enough on that. Don't send someone else to do something important. It did succeed in shaking you up, though." Andrew shrugged.

She was running out of questions, and that was all she had had to distract him from his mission. Her heart jumped into overdrive as she realized he was focusing on what he had brought her here to do again.

He stopped pacing and started toward her. "It's time we got on with this. I think you know everything you need to know."

He held up an ugly knife with a huge blade. The sound of waves lapping gently against a boat in the cove drew her attention as he advanced on her once more. Her breath caught and her blood chilled in her veins.

"You don't really want to do this. It makes you no better than my grandfather if you do." Even though he had already killed Natalie, she hoped for a twinge of conscience somehow. She didn't know how else to reason with him. He had the diamond. No one would be the wiser. He would get what he wanted after all.

Her pulse was thumping in her ears as red-hot fury

filled his face. She didn't know how else to distract him, to keep him talking. He glanced away, and her eyes fell toward the sand beneath her hands where she still knelt. It was cool to the touch, and suddenly she was struck with an idea. She surreptitiously grasped a handful of sand. Then she casually grasped another handful in the other hand, praying the whole time that he didn't see. She was thankful for the cover of darkness as a cloud passed over the moon for a brief moment.

He knelt before her to pull her back up to her feet, and at the same time, she saw another shadow shift, closer this time, as the moon reappeared from behind the clouds. Could it be Caldwell? Had he realized she was missing from the cottage and suspected where she might be? She swallowed back the tangle of emotions that had her both terrified and exhilarated that he might be here to help her. She took a deep, calming breath.

Whoever was out there, she prayed they had a gun. Counting to herself to try to remain patient until the right time, she clutched the sand carefully, trying not to let it run out the cracks in her clenched fists. She needed to keep hold of enough of it to do some damage.

Andrew tried to grab her hands, and she had to do something or she was going to lose the sand. She jerked away from him, and then reared back and threw it as hard as she could toward his face. It was awkward with her hands tied, but the spray of grit found its mark, and he let go of her to try and shield his eyes, but it was too late. He fell forward, the blade gliding painfully over her bare knee before falling into the sand.

Thrusting one leg out as she scrambled upward, she kicked him hard in the chest, throwing him off balance again.

She jumped to her feet and ran as fast as she could in

the deep sand. She screamed as loud as she could. "Help me! It's Andrew Siebert! He's trying to kill me!"

She heard him curse somewhere behind her, calling her every kind of unsavory name he could think of. She kept running, praying as she struggled through the sand at an excruciatingly slow pace. She sank deep into the soft beach with every stride, fighting the aching pain in her muscles just to keep going. She pushed herself forward with sheer determination, using every bit of strength she had left. The salty scent of ocean air was harsh in her nose as she struggled to breathe well enough to keep going.

She heard him start to run in her direction somewhere behind her, still not recovered from her retaliating on-slaught. Before he could catch up to her in his current state, though, she ran smack into a sturdy figure.

"I've got you," a voice said.

A pair of muscular arms clasped around her.

SIXTEEN

Jayde opened her mouth to scream, but he shushed her. "Hey, I'm on your side! I'm Caldwell's brother Avery!"

She calmed at once. "Where is he?"

"Sneaking around the other side to help Beau, Briggs and Grayson trap him." Avery grinned. "That was some smart thinking back there with the sand."

She nodded. "Thanks. Do you need to help? I'm fine."

He chuckled. "You look it."

When she gasped, he pointed to her bare feet and a trickle of blood running down her leg.

"It's just a scratch." She smiled at him. "And barefoot is the only way to be on the beach."

An agonized groan sounded from the other end of the beach then, drawing their attention.

Caldwell had tackled Andrew, forcing him onto the sand and just pulling his head up enough to keep him from suffocating.

"Admit what you've done! You're a dirty cop. You killed Natalie and tried to kill Jayde all for the sake of money." Caldwell's voice was full of anguish.

"You don't know the whole story. You're a fool for involving yourself with that family. They took everything from my family. Don't you see? I can't forgive them. They can't be trusted."

Caldwell jerked him up, though he was still squinting and blinking furiously from the gritty sand in his eyes. Jayde almost felt sorry for him.

"Did you frame Tristan for the whole thing, as well? For killing Natalie? For breaking into my home?" Caldwell's face was red. The veins stood out in his neck as he fought to remain calm.

"No. He was in on the whole thing. It was a combined effort. I swear." Andrew began sputtering, sure he could talk his way out of taking the brunt of Caldwell's fury.

"Who thought it all up?" Caldwell's voice was dead calm now. "Who capsized her boat?"

It was chilling. The fury was only present in his eyes. Andrew visibly shrank back.

"Tell me!" Caldwell shook him hard, and Andrew whimpered.

"It was me. I took care of it. Because Tristan couldn't. He told me he knew where the diamond was. He didn't know." He wrested his arms back and forth, trying to get loose, but Caldwell's latent anger gave him the strength of ten men.

"But you set him up so that he would be arrested tonight. You wanted to get us both out of the way so you could get to Jayde and take the diamond. Right?" Caldwell's voice sounded certain despite his question.

"Something like that. How does it feel, Thorpe? Right under your nose. You never once suspected me. All that time I worked with you, and you didn't even consider that I might have been involved. Your wife did, though. She found out who my grandfather was, and it was all over. She found Pierce, also. That helped her make the rest of the connections."

"So she wasn't in the cove that night because of the stone. She was there because of you." Anger tensed Caldwell's entire body.

"That's right. She agreed to meet with me about coming to an agreement. Tristan wanted to wait. I knew we needed to get her out of the way before she confided in you." Andrew's voice was triumphant despite the fact that he was obviously caught.

"How did she find out who your grandfather was?" Caldwell wanted to know everything.

"It was in the old journal she found leading her to the Rose Stone. Her grandfather identified my grandfather by name in the journal. He also mentioned that his grandson would be after the diamond if he ever suspected. It only took her a little genealogical research to find that grandson."

"And the journal? Where is it?"

"I burned it. You won't get your hands on it. I made your wife watch it burn just before I killed her."

The rage poured out of Caldwell then. He pinned Andrew down, pressing him into the sand.

"Easy, brother. You don't want to kill him. 'Vengeance is mine; I will repay, saith the Lord.' I'm not sure of the verse and the chapter, but in any case, it's best left to Him." One of the identical twins, though she didn't yet know the difference between Beau and Briggs, provided the voice of reason from behind Caldwell. "We'll let the judicial system see to it he doesn't do anything to harm anyone else until then."

Two other brothers, the other twin and another who must be Grayson, gently pulled Caldwell away and took charge of their captive. Avery nudged Jayde then, and she ran to Caldwell's side.

"I'm so glad you're safe." He pulled her into his arms.

Jayde pressed her face against his chest.

"I should've trusted my instincts. I knew there was more to the case. I should never have left you alone until I had it all figured out." He tilted her head back to look into her eyes. "I'm so sorry."

She shook her head. "You couldn't have known what he had planned. And you can't stay with me all the time."

He gave her a look that was far too serious and filled with all the emotion she had been fighting to let out herself. "I want to, though. I want to have every excuse to be with you as much as I possibly can for the rest of my life."

She could only stare back at him for a moment. "Do you mean what I think you mean?"

"If you think I mean I want to spend the rest of my life with you, then yes. I want you to be my wife, Jayde Cambrey. I want to marry you," he whispered so only she could hear. He was staring at her lips.

She felt the urge to tease him rise within her along with the giddiness that was filling her at his words.

"Hmm. I don't know. Your brother was awfully charming." She smiled broadly, letting him know she was only teasing.

"Hmm. Well. All my brothers are married. I'm the only one available. Sorry to disappoint you." He shrugged, but his own smile was just as big as hers.

"Well, I guess you'll do." She leaned in and kissed him then, and she did everything she could to leave no doubt at all about which Thorpe brother she really wanted.

Jayde couldn't believe how things had turned out.

All this time their attacker had known their every move because he was working in Caldwell's sheriff's department. It terrified her to think about how close Andrew had come to killing them both.

And then there was her cousin, Tristan.

It didn't make her feel any better at all that killing Natalie when he did was Andrew's idea and not Tristan's. She couldn't describe how violated and shaken she felt knowing that her own relative had wanted to harm them. It made nausea roil up in her stomach.

She had asked Caldwell if she could speak to her cousin for a moment when they arrived back at the station. Tristan had confessed to her that the animosity between Jayde's mother and the rest of the family stemmed from what they all knew. The three siblings had known about what their father had done all along. Jayde's mother had been the one to keep them from cashing in on the diamond and artifacts. She had rightfully disapproved and threatened to tell the whole story if they tried to profit from the stone. And she apparently had just enough evidence to keep them from doing so.

How she had kept the others from doing anything about it all this time, Jayde didn't understand.

She needed time to think.

She needed to talk to her mother, also. But it was late.

A couple of Caldwell's brothers had escorted her back to the beach cottage while he took Andrew Siebert in, and she had come straight to the guest bedroom alone. But she couldn't quite clear her head to think here.

Salty ocean air might do the trick.

She told Caldwell's brothers that she was just going to go for a quiet walk to clear her head, and they nodded, but followed her as far as the back deck to keep an eye on her surroundings. She appreciated the gesture, even though the threat really was over this time.

She had been disappointed to learn that her grandfather's journal had been destroyed, even though she now thought he had been a terrible man. Had he, or had he simply become overwhelmed by the glamor and lure of finding a hidden treasure?

She would have liked to have known how he found it, as well. Had he also been very brilliant? As a child, she hadn't given much thought to the extent of her grandfather's intelligence, but perhaps children always thought their parents and grandparents were brilliant.

No doubt her mother tried to convince him to admit to what he had done, to give up the diamond and make reparations. That was likely the true source of their discord.

But she wouldn't know until she spoke to her mother.

Caldwell didn't even want to part with Jayde long enough to take care of the captive, but he knew he had a job to do. Sometimes being the sheriff was a real pain in his backside.

That's why he was going to give it up.

That, and he was going to focus all his attentions on a certain female in his life.

There was still a lot they needed to work out. She had a life in Atlanta, and he didn't know how she felt about leaving it. He would follow her there if that's what she chose. But if he were honest with himself, he wanted more than anything to get back to his roots. Beau owned the family ranch now, but he knew there was property coming up for sale in the area where he grew up. He thought the idea of starting a small ranch of his own sounded fantastic.

He just wanted to get away from all the memories here and start fresh.

He had introduced all of his brothers to Jayde before sending them back to the beach house. They had promised to stay with her until he could get everything taken care of and get back. But he had really wanted to hand off his duties to someone else and stay with Jayde himself.

Ty offered to help however he could so that Caldwell could get back to her faster, but he couldn't just give it all to his deputy to handle. So they worked together to finish it as quickly as possible.

As they finished up, he asked Ty to come into his office to speak with him.

"I just want you to know I won't be seeking reelection when my term is up. I'm sure you have figured it out by now, though." Caldwell told Ty the news, but since it was only a little over a month out, he thought Ty was already aware of this fact.

"I'm sorry to hear that, sir. I wish you luck on your future endeavors, though." Ty gave a nod. "I had heard your name wouldn't be on the ballot, but I had hoped you might change your mind."

"I think my time here has come to an end." He couldn't keep the weariness from his voice. "But I hope one day you'll consider running for the position. You'd make a great sheriff."

Ty flushed. "I hope I'm able to do that someday. Thank you for your vote of confidence."

Caldwell nodded, and they both fell silent for a moment.

The paperwork was almost completed, and everything was settled concerning the two men who had caused Caldwell and Jayde such grief over the past few weeks. Ty waved Caldwell toward the door.

"Go on and check on your lady. I can finish up here." He grinned.

Caldwell didn't bother denying any of the insinuations in Ty's words. He hoped Jayde *was* his lady now. And he was definitely anxious to get back to her. "Thanks, Ty. For everything. You've been invaluable to me."

Again Ty flushed and nodded as Caldwell stood to go.

He made his way back to the cottage as quickly as he could, only to find Jayde wasn't even there.

"She said she needed a minute, bro. I think she's down on the beach." Avery gestured to the private beach area behind the cottage.

"Fine, I'll let her be." Caldwell sighed.

Caldwell looked around at his brothers, working on putting the mess in the house to rights. Avery looked so much more mature. Brigg and Beau wore matching contented expressions that made them look different, as well, and Grayson had that confident, settled look only a father could wear so well. He had missed them all so much.

He cleared his throat, and they all stopped what they were doing to look his way.

"I just want you all to know...you showing up like this means everything to me. I should never have turned my back on my family. I didn't deserve your help." They each made quips and jokes about his remark, but forgiveness was apparent in each of their expressions. Caldwell hugged each of them in turn.

Avery hugged him the tightest. "None of us deserve it, brother. That's just the thing. But no matter how far away you run, you never lose our love."

"Actually, I've been thinking about that." Caldwell cleared his throat. "I know you guys are scattered all over the country with your families, but I want to come home. Would anyone mind if I come back to Wyoming?"

"Why would any of us mind?" Beau clapped him on the back.

"Yeah, as long as you keep in touch with us from now on and show up for holidays, we can deal with wherever you want to live. And I'm considering retiring and moving closer to home myself." Grayson spoke up. "You have nieces and nephews to meet. Not to mention some gorgeous sisters-in-law."

Caldwell smiled. "I'm not sure how you all fooled anyone into getting married to you."

Groans and ornery remarks followed his comment.

"Where do you plan to live? Beau and Evie live at the ranch now. Will you stay there with them?" Avery was first to ask the question aloud, but they had all apparently been wondering. Murmurs and nods went around the room.

"No. I might ask to stay with them for a bit until I find us a suitable home, but I don't think my bride and I will want to share a home with this guy." He roughed up Beau's arm teasingly.

"Your bride?" Briggs spoke at last. "You asked her to marry you?"

Caldwell could feel the heat taking over his face. "Yeah."

"Thank goodness. I was afraid you weren't smart enough to ask her." Avery's remark earned him a pop in the arm.

"Enough. I know you haven't gotten beat up in a while, but it's too soon for you to start a fight." Grayson rolled his eyes at his joke.

"I want you all to know that I talked to Mom also. She's coming to the wedding." Caldwell had to choke out the words. "When I told her I forgave her, she sobbed. I really should have done it much sooner."

The brothers surrounded him in a hug.

"You needed time. It's okay." Briggs gave him a single nod and the other brothers followed suit.

"I have one question, though. What about the island?

Don't you own practically all of it?" Avery tilted his head in curiosity.

"Not anymore. I signed most of it over to the National Park Service. I offered to give it to Jayde's parents, but she told me she'd rather it not belong to any individual or family. She said everyone should be able to enjoy it. I decided she was right." Caldwell swallowed hard. It had been a difficult decision. But he didn't want to be here anymore and neither did Jayde.

"Wow. That's a lot of property to just give away. The rentals, the land, everything." Grayson frowned.

"I should have a tax credit for a very long time." He grinned sheepishly.

"Can you give up your job as sheriff so easily?" Briggs asked.

"My term is up next month, anyway, actually. I'd already decided against running for reelection. It all sort of lined up for me."

"I'd say that's God at work." Beau pushed his hat up on his head a bit. Caldwell could see his forehead was sweating. He was accustomed to the cool, dry climates of Wyoming.

"So you'll need a job?" Avery asked.

"I was thinking of getting back to my roots. I'd like to go back to riding and ranching, maybe raising some good horses," Caldwell explained.

"Funny, I was looking for a partner to do something along these lines myself." Avery grinned. "I'll keep working as a PI, but I'd like to do more. I wonder if we could somehow coordinate our business plans. Any interest in investigating in the private sector, Sheriff?"

"It might be a possibility." Caldwell offered his hand to shake, and Avery grasped it and pulled him in for a hug.

"I've sure missed my brother." Avery gave him a

squeeze. "I'm sorry for the disagreement. I won't say it'll never happen again, but I promise to never react that way again."

"I've missed you, too, and I promise not to react so poorly again, either." Caldwell grinned.

Caldwell had a sensation come over him just then of the gloom lifting, as if the sun had just come out after an extended period of heavy cloud cover.

SEVENTEEN

Jayde continued to wander along the beach for another half hour, carrying her shoes in her hand. She stared out at the water hoping for some wisdom to float her way. She loved Caldwell with all her heart. But was she making the right decision? She had worked so hard for a career that had never really satisfied her, and she couldn't see Caldwell ever being happy in Atlanta.

So she planned to give it up.

Whether they stayed here or moved somewhere else, like back to Wyoming where he had grown up, she knew her place was with him.

The sand was cool on her feet, and she considered the moon shining on the water. It was late and she needed to get some sleep. Maybe she could think more clearly about the whole situation in the morning.

But even as she had the thought, her heart reassured her she would never be more confident of one thing.

She wanted to spend the rest of her life with Caldwell Thorpe.

As if her thoughts had brought him to her, his shadow appeared down the beach a ways. She knew it was him from the athletic way he moved, as if the sand was no more than a little bit of grass around his feet. His silhouette looked as strong and steady as the man himself, and her heart did a little flip in her chest as she stopped to wait for his approach.

He paused before her as he reached her at last, and any lingering doubts she might have had about rushing into this relationship fled. He smiled before pulling her to him. "We have so much to talk about."

"Yes, we do." She wrapped her arms around him and let him hold her there on the beach in the moonlight. "Everything happened so fast."

He put just a bit of space between them so he could look into her face. "You're not having doubts, are you?"

The hurt expression in his eyes made her want to say no. But she owed him the truth. "To be honest, for a second there I wondered if I was jumping into things too quickly. But then I saw you and I knew it was right. You're everything I've ever wanted. I love you with my whole heart."

His brows furrowed for a second, but as she continued her explanation, he relaxed. He pulled her close to his chest and smoothed her hair away from her face. Then he leaned down and kissed her forehead. "Thank goodness. When my brothers said that you needed a minute, I was afraid you had changed your mind. Then you were gone for so long…"

She shook her head where it was cradled against him. "No, definitely not."

"Good. Because I love you more than I have ever loved anyone. I don't want you ever thinking because I was married before that you're taking second place." He stroked her hair again.

She sucked in a breath. She *had* been afraid of that, hadn't she? And yet he was reassuring her that it wasn't so without her even mentioning her fears. "I won't say that hasn't been a concern for me. My former boyfriend certainly never made me first. He wrecked my trust, and I worried that you might not truly be over Natalie and everything that happened to her."

"Well, it shouldn't be a concern. I'm sorry that he took advantage of you, but there is no one else in my heart. I know it must be weird that Natalie was your cousin. But when I look at you, you're all I see, Jayde. I don't think of Natalie at all. You're a totally different person, and while I did love Natalie, what I feel for you is altogether different. I want you to understand there will be no competition between you." He spoke softly and close to her ear. The warmth of his breath was comforting and reassuring.

She tightened her arms around him and smiled up at him. "I'm really glad to hear that."

"You don't have to take me at my word, either. I'll spend the rest of my life proving it to you." His heart was beating with strength where she was pressed against him in his embrace, and it reassured her somehow.

"I like the sound of that." Jayde laid a hand on his chest where his heart was beating below her cheek.

Caldwell walked down to the beach again later the next afternoon to let Jayde make the phone call to her mother she had been so dreading. He understood her fear, but more, her sadness at having to tell them what her cousin had done. She had been exhausted from the long night before, however, so he had encouraged her to sleep before taking on that task.

He considered all that had happened in the past few days with a deep sigh of thanks to the Lord. He was reconciled with his family. He had called his mother again this morning while Jayde slept and begun trying to make up for the losses in their relationship. Things would be fragile for a while, but there was the hope borne of forgiveness between them now. His relief at no longer having discord between himself and his family was nearly palpable, and he felt like a new man.

When Jayde came strolling down the beach toward him, he could see that she had been crying, but her expression was one of relief, as well. She paused before him and smiled.

"Well, it was a lot of information I didn't really want to hear, but at least I know the truth now."

Caldwell folded her into his arms and kissed her forehead. "You've been through a lot. You don't have to tell me right now if you don't want to."

Jayde sighed. "I'd rather have it over with while it's on my mind, anyway."

He settled them both into chairs in the sand. He took her hand and waited, wanting her to speak her piece in her own time.

"I understand now why my family was so distant with one another. Most of them were apparently consumed with the love of money. My grandfather was a thief and a crook. He learned about the legend not long after buying the island of Deadman's Cay and hired Siebert's grandfather, an archaeologist by the name of Caleb Hartman, as his partner to help him search. He hired a man to steal the artifacts from the museum, and they began their search. But after months of digging up clues, Grandfather figured it out first. He found the diamond in the cove—in the very cave Andrew Siebert took it back to. It was hidden beneath what's believed to be a pirate's grave, and when he found it first, alone, he killed his partner and put it back there, intending to retrieve it later. He didn't think anyone would disturb the grave to look there, which is probably along the lines of what the pirates thought, as well."

She took a deep breath but continued.

"His partner's daughter, however, had seen the murder transpire. But she was young and afraid, and my grandfather threatened her. Jessica Hartman kept the secret, or so he thought, to save herself and the rest of her family. She was Andrew Siebert's mother."

Caldwell drew in a breath. "Wow."

"Exactly. It gets worse. Jessica Hartman was a friend of my mother's growing up, but after it happened, Jessica shunned my mother, although my mother didn't know why for many years. Jessica groomed Andrew to one day take revenge on our family, making sure to keep it all a secret so no one would suspect. When word got out that Natalie had begun to look for the diamond, he felt it was time to take action. Whether or not Natalie actually sent him a letter is all speculation. I don't think so because he said she claimed to want to give everyone their share. But she never contacted our family."

"And your family didn't know anything about this the whole time?" Caldwell's brows furrowed in the bright sunshine as the water lapped peacefully on the shore.

"Yes, actually, they did. Sometime a few years before his death, my grandfather confessed to his children. His wife had already passed on, and he wanted them to be the ones to get to the stone, in the event that Jessica Hartman tried to find it. But his memory began to slip, and he couldn't tell them where it was by the time he made his full confession. He had also misplaced the journal that Natalie later found. My mother was horrified by what he had done, though, and insisted he confess to the authorities and turn it all in, but her siblings wanted the money. They couldn't come to an agreement, other than not to tell the grandchildren. That's why Natalie, Tristan and I didn't know."

She paused and peered out across the water for a moment, squeezing his hand.

"This is unreal. Why didn't your mother just go to the authorities herself?" Caldwell followed her eyes across the water before turning back to look at her face.

"She tried. But apparently Tristan's mother, Felicity, threatened to kill her if she didn't keep her mouth shut. Perhaps that's where Tristan's violent streak came from. Anyway, Natalie's father backed Felicity. Phillip, Natalie's father, wanted them to team up and go find the stone. My mother wouldn't do it. She told them all they were a bunch of criminals, but she couldn't do anything about it because of their threats. And there was still a chance Jessica Hartman might come after them, as well. But my mother had the one thing that could keep her siblings from finding the diamond and cashing in on it without her."

"What was that?" Caldwell couldn't imagine how she had kept them from going after it without her.

"The deed to the cove. If you look at your deed, you will see that there is a tiny piece of land there that isn't part of your property. It's marked as unknown. If anyone else tried to claim the diamond found there, she could sue them. They couldn't claim ownership of anything found there in the cove without her."

"But the diamond was in the cottage." Caldwell wasn't quite comprehending how this story was unfolding.

"Yes, it was when we found it. But only because Natalie had put it there. She didn't know, see. Because they never told the grandchildren. And my mother has documentation signed by my grandfather saying that it was found there. Apparently legally, she's the only one in the family who could sell it, but only with signed agreements from her siblings. My grandfather set it all up carefully so that none of them could claim it alone. They would have to work together to profit from the diamond, and my mother refused." Jayde smiled. "I can't help being proud of her for it."

"You should be. I'm sure it would've been very easy to just give in and take the money. Even if they did have Jessica Hartman to worry about." Caldwell squeezed her hand.

"She's no longer living. And it seems a little unfair that her son is going to spend the rest of his life in prison after what my grandfather did." Jayde sighed. "I don't know how to make amends."

Caldwell stood. "Some things are best left in God's hands. You didn't have anything to do with Hartman's death. But his grandson killed Natalie and tried to kill you. You've relinquished the diamond, the artifacts, all of it to the museum. That should be enough."

"My mother thinks her siblings will be angry once they find out what's happened. I'm more concerned for Tristan's parents and their mental well-being." Jayde took the hand Caldwell stretched out toward her and rose to her feet.

"What did your father have to say about all of this?" Caldwell asked.

"He's always backed my mother one hundred percent on everything. She put the phone on speaker for a few minutes so he could say hello. He promised me he would protect her, just as he always has. He would never say or do anything to hurt her, nor will he let her siblings hurt her. He's a good man. Just like you, Caldwell Thorpe."

She relaxed into his arms then, having released the last of her upset over the story of her family's past. She vowed to follow in her mother's footsteps, though. Honesty and integrity in all things, as much as was within her control.

"You're a good woman, too, Jayde Cambrey. And I can't wait to make you mine forever." He wrapped her tightly in his arms. She sighed and melted into his embrace.

He silenced any reply she might have uttered with a tender, loving kiss.

EPILOGUE

Caldwell took Jayde back to Wyoming a few months later. She immediately fell in love with the wild landscape, even though it was winter and the snow was coming so often there wasn't a lot of landscape to see. Her boss at the advertising firm in Atlanta had let her go reluctantly but helped her find a part-time remote position until she decided what she wanted to do with her future.

Tristan and Andrew had each turned on the other, and they had both ended up serving extensive prison time for their crimes. Jayde had been deeply hurt by her cousin's betrayal, but Caldwell had done everything he could to keep her mind off it. The rest of the family had accepted that the Rose Stone was gone for good, and it seemed to have lifted a great deal of the tension that had been lingering between them.

Caldwell and Jayde had decided to keep the cottage and a little bit of the land on Deadman's Cay just for the family's use and possible vacations. The rest had gone to public use under the ownership of the state parks and wildlife division. The ownership of the cove had also gone to the museum when Jayde's mother learned what they had planned to do. Since pirates had once used it for a lair, they all agreed it should be explored and preserved as part of the island's dark history, considering there might be other artifacts contained in its depths.

Jayde and Caldwell married the next summer on the Thorpe family ranch with all of Caldwell's brothers present. His mother was there, as well, considering she and Caldwell had finally made peace with one another. Jayde's parents were thrilled to visit the Wyoming ranch for a few days, and to her surprise, Tristan's parents even came to the wedding. They apologized and asked Jayde to forgive them all, and Jayde readily agreed, though she knew Tristan would still pay for his crimes.

In addition to Caldwell's brothers and sisters-in-law, Jayde wanted to include their tiny nieces and nephews in the wedding, and they carried a runner of flowers. Riley, being the oldest, led the way down the aisle to the couple before standing with their parents alongside Jayde and Caldwell. Briggs and Madison's daughter, Livie Rose, was next. After her came the two boys, toddling along about the same size. Lauren and Grayson had named their son Nash, while Avery and Brynn's son had been named Ian. Both were barely toddling, so Evie's sister, Mia, now almost twelve, helped guide them along. And Mia was thrilled, of course, at the announcement that Evie and Beau would be having a child of their own before fall set in. According to the ultrasound, another girl would be added to the family this time, and they hoped to name her Mallory Clare. Avery informed Caldwell that he had some catching up to do, making Jayde blush.

The ceremony was short, with Jayde's father giving her away while her mother looked on tearfully. A few friends from Atlanta made it to the wedding, but most importantly, Jayde felt the peace and approval from her cousin in her heart, as if Natalie looked on with great satisfaction at how things had turned out. It had taken

Jayde a couple of months to reconcile her own concerns with the circumstances, but Caldwell's unconditional love had helped her through it. They were both so happy and content together that she realized letting anything come between them was a terrible mistake.

Caldwell found a piece of land for sale not far from his brothers, Beau and Avery, in Wyoming, where he built a beautiful home for Jayde. It would slowly become an operational ranch, as well, though on a much smaller scale than Beau and Evie's place. Jayde surprised him by knowing how to ride and care for horses, and she picked up on ranching life very quickly, much to her new sisters-in-law's collective delight. They rode together often in the weeks leading up to the wedding, and Caldwell spent that time making up for lost moments with his brothers.

By the time the preacher had pronounced them man and wife, Caldwell's heart was so full he thought it might burst. He looked around at his family, then back at the woman he loved with his entire heart and let out a whoop as he ended their first kiss as husband and wife.

"What was that about?" Jayde laughed.

He responded first by kissing her again, though he had already followed the preacher's directive. "If I didn't let some of this happiness out, I was afraid I might explode."

His explanation brought smiles and laughter to everyone in the audience.

"I didn't know that would help. In that case... Woo-hoo!"

Jayde's joyous exclamation brought more laughter, and before they knew it, the entire Thorpe family and all their friends surrounding them let out a whoop of their own.

* * * * *

If you liked this story from Sommer Smith,
check out her previous
Love Inspired Suspense books,

Under Suspicion
Attempted Abduction
Ranch Under Siege
Wyoming Cold Case Secrets
Wyoming Ranch Ambush

Available now from Love Inspired Suspense!

Find more great reads at www.LoveInspired.com.

Dear Reader,

Thank you for choosing this book! If you've been following along with the Thorpe brothers' other stories, you know that Caldwell has been a bit of an outsider among them. His difficulty with forgiving his mother became a source of tension and discord, and he decided to take his own path. But with her gentle nature and easy trust, Jayde helped Caldwell see that life is too short to bear a grudge. I was so glad to see him reconciled with his family. I hope you found this to be a satisfying conclusion to the stories about these five strong men. I have always wanted to write a story with pirates involved!

Wishing you all the best!
Sommer Smith

COMING NEXT MONTH FROM
Love Inspired Suspense

BABY PROTECTION MISSION
Mountain Country K-9 Unit • by Laura Scott

When his sister is abducted, rancher Cade McNeal will do anything to keep his newborn nephew safe from a kidnapper's clutches. But as danger escalates, he'll need Officer Ashley Hanson and her K-9 partner to help evade the assailants on their tail and find his sister...*before* time runs out.

TRACKING THE TRUTH
Security Hounds Investigations • by Dana Mentink

After Emery Duncan is kidnapped and dumped in a lake, Roman Wolfe and his bloodhound rescue her from an icy death. Someone doesn't want her to find out what really happened the night her father confessed to attempted murder. Can Roman protect Emery and her baby nephew long enough to discover the truth?

COLD CASE TARGET
Texas Crime Scene Cleaners • by Jessica R. Patch

Sissy Spencer finds herself in a killer's crosshairs after she walks in on a man trying to murder her friend. When her ex-boyfriend, private investigator Beau Brighton, saves her, she knows she must rely on him to stay alive. Only protecting Sissy becomes a dangerous game when they unravel her terrifying connection to a serial killer...

ROCKY MOUNTAIN SURVIVAL
by Jane M. Choate

Someone's willing to kill for photojournalist Kylie Robertson's photos. After she's attacked, she flees to the only person she trusts—her ex, former navy SEAL Josh Harvath. Can they piece together the mystery behind the images *and* their past...or will they fall victim to unknown enemies?

TREACHEROUS ESCAPE
by Kellie VanHorn

Biochemist Vienna Clayton makes a groundbreaking discovery—and now she's framed for her boss's murder, her laptop is stolen and gunmen are after her. She escapes, but park ranger Hudson Lawrence saves her when her boat is capsized. Together, they must clear her name and uncover the true culprits...before she's silenced for good.

COLORADO DOUBLE CROSS
by Jennifer Pierce

Determined to prove his partner's death was a setup, DEA agent Nick Anderson goes undercover in a drug cartel. Only now he and his partner's widow, Alexis White, are caught up in a lethal web of deception, corruption and murder...and they could be the next to die.

LOOK FOR THESE AND OTHER LOVE INSPIRED BOOKS WHEREVER BOOKS ARE SOLD, INCLUDING MOST BOOKSTORES, SUPERMARKETS, DISCOUNT STORES AND DRUGSTORES.

LISCNM0224